24

Universal Economics and the Song of the Elders

Tai-Zamarai Yasharahyalah

24 : Universal Economics and the Song of the Elders
Book formatting by Tai-Zamarai Yasharahyalah

Copyright © 2024 by Tai-Zamarai Yasharahyalah
B3 MAGNAT3®

All rights reserved. Printed in the United Kingdom. No part of this book may be used or reproduced in any manner whatsoever without written permission except in the case of brief quotations em- bodied in critical articles or reviews.
Though elements of this book are Non-fiction, Names, characters, businesses, organiza- tions, places, events and incidents are used either as resemblance of real life events and situations or are purely fictitious. Any resemblance to actual persons not intended, living or dead, events, or locales is entirely coincidental.

Instagram, Facebook and YouTube Handle :
@B3.FR33

Book and Cover design by Tai-Zamarai Yasharahyalah
©B3 MAGNAT3

First Edition : July 2024

Prologue

The Genesis of Creation

The 12th Realm, also known as the Genesis Plane, exists beyond the fabric of conventional reality. It is a realm of pure energy and infinite potential, where time and space intertwine in a symphony of creation. The realm is bathed in a radiant, ever-changing light, with colors that defy description and landscapes that shift like dreams. The 24 Elders of the 12th Dimension sing their ancient songs, resonating through the cosmos. On Earth, select scientists and spiritual leaders receive these songs, their hearts and minds tasked with deciphering the profound messages. However, the true intentions of CERN's experiments are revealed, leading to chaos. It's up to Priestess Amina and her initiates to appease the Elders and restore balance.

The Founding of the 12th Realm

In the beginning, before the stars were born and galaxies spun into existence, there was the Genesis Plane. The Architect, the Luminary, the Herald, and the Custodian gathered in the heart of this plane to bring forth a new creation.

24: Universal Economics and the Song of the Elders

The Architect: "From the void, we shall craft a realm of boundless potential, where the essence of creation can flourish. This will be the cradle of the multiverse."

The Luminary: "Our wisdom and energy will infuse this realm, giving birth to dimensions of infinite possibility. Here, the seeds of existence will be sown."

The Herald: "Let it be known across the cosmos: The Genesis Plane is the wellspring of all that is and all that will be. Iwala-- the laws of creation will govern this sacred space."

The Custodian: "I shall guard this realm and ensure the balance and harmony of the twelve dimensions. Each realm will reflect a facet of existence, interconnected yet unique."

The Source and Origins

The light within the Genesis Plane intensifies, forming a luminous core from which the energy of creation emanates. This core, known as the Source, is the heart of the 12th Realm.

24: Universal Economics and the Song of the Elders

The Architect: "The Source is the wellspring of all creation. Its energy is the lifeblood of the multiverse, flowing through the twelve realms and beyond."

The Luminary: "From this energy, we shall weave the fabric of reality. Each realm will draw from the Source, shaping its own unique existence."

The Herald: "The origins of this realm lie in the convergence of our energies and wills. We are the architects of reality, and our vision will guide the growth of the multiverse."

The Custodian: "And so, the twelve realms will be born, each a reflection of the Source, each a part of the whole. Our stewardship will ensure their harmony and growth."

Requirements for Ascension

The scene shifts to a gathering of higher beings, each representing different facets of wisdom, strength, and virtue. They stand before the Custodian, who holds the Universal Charter – a set of laws and principles governing the 12th Realm.

24: Universal Economics and the Song of the Elders

The Custodian: "To ascend to the Genesis Plane and partake in the creation of new realities, beings must embody the virtues of purity, wisdom, courage, and compassion. These are the pillars upon which our realm stands."

Ahia Aya | Ah (Higher Being 1): "Purity of heart ensures that the energies of creation are used for the greater good, untainted by selfish desires."

Ahia Aya | Ba (Higher Being 2): "Wisdom guides the application of these energies, ensuring that each creation is harmonious and balanced."

Ahia Aya | Ga (Higher Being 3): "Courage is necessary to face the unknown and embrace the infinite possibilities that the Genesis Plane offers."

Ahia Aya | Da (Higher Being 4): "Compassion binds us together, fostering unity and cooperation among the beings of the multiverse."

The Custodian: "Those who seek to ascend must undergo the Process – They must first descend. They must undertake a series of trials that test these virtues. Only by proving their worth can they join us in shaping the fabric of reality."

The Architect: "The Process is rigorous, but necessary. It ensures that only the most dedicated and virtuous beings can partake in the creation and stewardship of the multiverse."

24: Universal Economics and the Song of the Elders

The Luminary: "And so, the call will go out to the realms, inviting those who seek ascension to embark on this sacred journey and transcend all their limitations. The trials will test their essence, and their success will herald a new era of creation."

The Initiation of the Custodians

The scene shifts again, this time to a grand ceremony where new custodians of the twelve realms are being initiated. The air is thick with anticipation and reverence.

The Custodian: "As new custodians, you are the protectors and guides of your respective realms. You will oversee the balance and growth, ensuring that the energy of the Source flows freely and harmoniously."

New Custodian 1: "We accept this responsibility with humility and determination. We will uphold the principles of the Universal Charter and dedicate ourselves to the welfare of our realms."

*New Custodian 2***:** "Our journey has prepared us for this role. We are ready to face the challenges and embrace the opportunities that lie ahead."

24: Universal Economics and the Song of the Elders

The Architect: "Remember, you are not alone in this endeavor. The unity of the twelve realms depends on our collective efforts and collaboration."

The Luminary: "Your wisdom and virtue will guide you. Trust in the process and in each other, for together, we can achieve the extraordinary."

The Herald: "By the decree of the Universal Charter, you are now custodians of the twelve realms. May your journey be filled with light and your actions guided by the Source."

The Genesis Plane

A realm of radiant, ever-changing light, with landscapes that shift like dreams. The Source, a luminous core of pure energy, stands at the heart of this realm, emanating the essence of creation.

Ahia Aya (The Collective 'I am'): A solemn assembly of beings representing various virtues, standing before the Custodian who holds the Universal Charter.

Initiation Ceremony: A grand and reverent event where new custodians are initiated, surrounded by the ethereal beauty of the Genesis Plane and the presence of higher beings.

In the Genesis Plane, the 12th Realm is observed as the wellspring of creation and the heart of the multiverse. It highlights the founding of the realm by Chi Akwa Akaka-- the Architect, Chi Na Aka--the Luminary, Iwala--the Herald, and Ahia Aya--the Custodians/Higher Beings, and explains the Source as the core of creation. The requirements for ascension are detailed, emphasizing the virtues of purity, wisdom, courage, and compassion, and the rigorous Process that tests these virtues. The initiation of new custodians underscores the responsibility and unity required to maintain the harmony and growth of the twelve realms and in the exploration of the multiverse.

The Discovery of the 12th Dimension

Geneva, Switzerland. The CERN laboratory, home to the Large Hadron Collider. Scientists are gathered around a computer screen displaying unusual data.

The laboratory is buzzing with excitement. Dr. Tanis and Dr. Dubois are analyzing the data, while Dr. Wang joins them via a video call from China.

24: Universal Economics and the Song of the Elders

Dr. Tanis: "These readings are unprecedented. We've detected a particle that doesn't conform to any known physical laws."

Dr. Dubois: "Could it be a link to another dimension? The 12th dimension?"

Dr. Wang: "I've run the simulations here in Beijing. The energy signatures match those theorized for higher-dimensional interactions."

Dr. Tanis: "We need to confirm this with more experiments. If true, this could redefine our understanding of the universe."

The Initiation of the Custodians

A hidden ancient temple in Enugu, Southeast Nigeria. The temple is adorned with intricate carvings and symbols representing the cosmos.

The temple is dimly lit by torches. High Priestess Amina stands before the initiates, who kneel in a semicircle.

High Priestess Amina: "You have been chosen as the custodians of the 12 realms. Each of you represents a vital link in the chain that binds our universe."

24: Universal Economics and the Song of the Elders

Initiate 1 (from Kenya): "What is our purpose, High Priestess?"

High Priestess Amina: "To protect and preserve the balance of the realms. You will each receive the knowledge of your ancestors and the power to traverse dimensions."

The initiates bow their heads as the High Priestess performs the initiation ritual.

The Process - The Extraction

Stonehenge, Salisbury Plains, Wiltshire, England. The ancient stones stand against a backdrop of a setting sun. Elder Shamar and Zam Zam stand in the center of the stone circle, the air thick with anticipation.

Elder Shamar: "The Process of Extraction is not to be taken lightly. You will experience a separation of your essence from your physical form."

Zam Zam: "I'm ready. I've prepared for this my whole life."

Elder Shamar: "Focus on the stones. Let their ancient energy guide you."

Zam Zam closes his eyes, and a glowing aura begins to surround him. His body remains still, but his consciousness starts to drift towards the 12th dimension.

The Law of Governance and the Universal Charter

A grand hall in Kinshasa, Democratic Republic of the Congo. The hall is filled with representatives from each of the 12 regions.

The delegates are seated around a large circular table, each with a copy of the Universal Charter before them.

President Lumumba: "The Universal Charter outlines the laws of governance for all beings in the 12 realms. It is our duty to uphold these laws and ensure harmony across dimensions."

Delegate from Arkansas, USA: "How do we enforce these laws? There are forces beyond our control."

President Lumumba: "With unity and vigilance. The custodians among us will act as our intermediaries, ensuring that the balance is maintained."

The delegates nod in agreement, understanding the gravity of their responsibility.

24: Universal Economics and the Song of the Elders

Intergalactic Transactions and The Call

A bustling market in Kinshasa, where interstellar goods are traded. The market is vibrant with colors, sounds, and smells from different worlds.

Trader Kofi stands behind his stall, showcasing exotic items from different dimensions. Mari approaches, intrigued.

Mari: "What are these? I've never seen anything like them."

Trader Kofi: "These are artifacts from other realms. Each has its own story and power."

Mari: "How do you acquire them?"

Trader Kofi: "Through intergalactic transactions. There are portals on Earth that connect us to the cosmos. Only a few know their locations."

Mari picks up a glowing crystal, feeling a strange connection to it.

Trader Kofi: "Careful with that one. It responds to the heart's desires."

The Universal Intermediaries and The Song of the 24 Elders

24: Universal Economics and the Song of the Elders

A serene, otherworldly realm where the 24 Elders reside. The environment is filled with a harmonious melody that seems to resonate with the soul.

The Elders sit in a circle, their auras glowing brightly. The Song of the 24 Elders fills the air, a celestial harmony that binds the multiverse.

Elder Kaiyahla: "The mortals are on the brink of discovery. We must ensure they understand the gravity of their actions."

Elder Ahrayah: "Their intentions are pure, but their knowledge is limited. We must guide them."

Elder Zadaq: "If they misuse their newfound power, the consequences could be catastrophic."

Elder Kaiyahla: "We will send them a guide. One who can bridge the gap between their world and ours."

The Elders chant, and a beam of light emerges, heading towards Earth, signaling **The Call**.

The custodians are tasked with maintaining the balance of the realms. As the ancient and modern intersections of this responsibility reverberates through settings in Switzerland, Nigeria, England, the Congo, and more. The Universal Charter is established, outlining the laws of governance for the 12 realms. We see the beginnings of intergalactic transactions and the involvement of everyday people, hinting at the profound connections between Earth and the cosmos. The 24 Elders, are introduced who provide guidance and issue The Call to selected individuals on Earth, setting the stage for the unfolding journey into the unknown.

24: Universal Economics and the Song of the Elders

Basalt Relief of King Kilamiwwa from the 9th Century Showing Phoenician Writing

24: Universal Economics and the Song of the Elders

Song | 1

Uncharted Spaces

The First Song Received

CERN, Switzerland

Dr. Jean-Luc Dubois receives the first song during a late-night experiment.

The song's ancient language baffles the scientists.

A sudden, inexplicable energy surge occurs in the lab.

Jean-Luc: "This... this isn't just noise. It's like a message, but in a language I've never seen."

Alara: "I've heard ancient scripts before, but this is beyond anything known. We must decipher it."

Mei: "The energy readings are off the charts. What have we tapped into?"

24: Universal Economics and the Song of the Elders

24: Universal Economics and the Song of the Elders

Transliteration

Aka

Ihai nkai awkikai na-akpaw n'awchichiri

Kpakpandiw ka a miwriw n'imai aghiri ainwaighi ngwiwcha.

Mkpiwriw awbi na-atiwghari n'abiw aibighi aibi,

Awkiw nkai ndiw na-ainwiw gbaa.

Igbo Translation

Aka

Ìhè nke okike na-akpọ n'ọchịchịrị,

Kpakpando ka a mụrụ n'ime oghere enweghị ngwụcha.

Mkpụrụ obi na-atụgharị n'abụ ebighi ebi,

Ọkụ nke ndụ na-enwu gbaa.

English Translation:

Aka

Light of creation calls in the dark,

Stars are born in the infinite void.

Souls resonate in an eternal song,

The flame of life shines brightly.

Introduction to the Elders

The Council Chamber in the 12th Dimension

The Council Chamber of the 12th Dimension is a place of transcendental grandeur, suspended in an endless expanse of shimmering light and cascading stars. The chamber itself is a perfect circle, with walls made of translucent crystal that refract light into a spectrum of colors, creating a living rainbow that dances around the room. At the centre lies a large, circular table carved from a single piece of sapphire stone, with living, moving wheels made of beryl. Its surface is engraved with ancient runes that pulse with a gentle, steady glow.

24: Universal Economics and the Song of the Elders

Around this dynamic table sit the 24 Elders, each a radiant being representing one of the realms within the 12th Dimension. Their appearances are as varied as the realms they govern, each exuding an aura of wisdom and power.

Elder Mmbagwiw, the Keeper of Light, has an appearance that embodies purity and brightness. Her form is enveloped in a robe of shimmering white, and her eyes shine with a golden light that speaks of ages of knowledge.

Elder Nkwa, the Master of Winds, appears as a translucent figure, constantly shifting like a gentle breeze. His voice carries the whisper of the wind, calm and soothing.

Elder Nnshimiri, the Guardian of Oceans, has a form that seems to flow like water, her robes undulating in waves of deep blue and green. Her presence brings a sense of tranquility and depth.

Elder Abaraka, the Wielder of Flames, radiates warmth and energy. His form is a blaze of fiery hues, and his eyes burn with an intensity that can be both comforting and intimidating.

The remaining Elders, each with their unique attributes and realms, form a circle of balance and harmony, their combined energies creating a powerful and serene atmosphere.

24: Universal Economics and the Song of the Elders

Elder Mmbagwiw: (voice resonating with light) "The multiverse trembles. The balance of power shifts like never before. We must address these changes with utmost urgency."

Elder Nkwa: (whispering with the wind) "Indeed, the winds carry whispers of unrest. Many realms report disturbances in their natural order."

Elder Nnshimiri: (calm and deep) "The oceans reveal currents of discontent. The harmony we have long maintained is at risk. We must act to restore balance."

Elder Abaraka: (fiery and intense) "The flames of discord burn brighter. Conflict brews in places once peaceful. We need a strategy to quell these disturbances."

Elder Saraphina: (a being of ethereal grace) "Our first priority is understanding the source. What has caused such a profound imbalance across the dimensions?"

Elder Achichi: (a figure of celestial strength) "Our scouts have reported unusual activities in the lower dimensions. Entities of unknown origin exert influence and disrupt the natural order."

Elder Mmbagwiw: "Then we must send envoys to these realms. Our presence alone may suffice to restore harmony. If not, we shall use our combined wisdom to guide them back to the light."

24: Universal Economics and the Song of the Elders

Elder Nkwa: "I volunteer to visit the realms of air. My presence will soothe the storms and bring clarity."

Elder Nnshimiri: "And I shall journey to the water realms. The seas must know tranquility once more."

Elder Abaraka: "I will take the fire realms. They respond to strength and will follow if led with power."

Elder Saraphina: "Together, we shall address this crisis. Each of us must use our unique abilities to restore balance. We cannot afford to fail."

Elder Achichi: "Agreed. Let us prepare and begin our journey. The fate of the multiverse depends on our actions."

As the Elders rise from their seats, their combined energies create a radiant burst of light that fills the chamber. Each Elder prepares to embark on their mission, knowing that the harmony of the multiverse rests in their hands. Their unity and wisdom will be the key to restoring balance and ensuring the continued prosperity of all realms.

Quantum Links to the 12 Multiverse

CERN Laboratory, Geneva, Switzerland. A high-tech laboratory filled with advanced equipment. A blend of cutting-edge technology and scientific instruments, with a sterile and organized atmosphere. The holographic displays cast a blue glow, illuminating the faces of the scientists. The lab is buzzing with activity, with scientists working on various high-tech equipment.

Laboratory: A blend of cutting-edge technology and scientific instruments, with a sterile and organized atmosphere. The room is filled with the hum of machinery and the glow of holographic displays, and scientists in white coats and the occasional beep of monitors. The walls are adorned with charts depicting the multiverse.

Dr. Tanis and Dr. Dubois stand in front of a large holographic screen displaying complex equations and a 3D model of the multiverse. Dr. Wang appears on a video call screen beside them.

Dr. Tanis: "We've finally mapped the quantum links. These connections suggest that the 12th dimension is not just theoretical—it's real."

Dr. Dubois: "The energy signatures are unlike anything we've seen before. It's as if they're calling to us."

24: Universal Economics and the Song of the Elders

Dr. Wang: *via video call* "In Beijing, we've replicated the experiment. The results are consistent. We might be looking at a stable bridge between dimensions."

Ida: "But how do we ensure safe travel through these links? The theoretical risks are immense."

ALPHA: "The universal intermediaries, described in ancient texts, may provide the stability needed. Their presence could stabilize the link."

Dr. Tanis: "The 'Song of the 24 Elders'—it's more than a myth. We need to decode it. It could be the key to harnessing the power of the intermediaries."

Dr. Tanis: "The quantum links we've discovered connect us to the 12th dimension. This isn't just theory anymore; it's reality."

Professor Sloane: "We've mapped these connections, but entering the 12th dimension remains elusive. The energy requirements are astronomical."

Ida: "What about the universal intermediaries? Could they help stabilize the link?"

ALPHA: "The universal intermediaries, as described in the ancient texts, serve as bridges between dimensions. If we can harness their power, we might achieve stable entry."

24: Universal Economics and the Song of the Elders

Dr. Tanis: "The 24 Elders are said to be the custodians of these intermediaries. We need to decode their 'Song'—it's believed to be the key."

They all turn to a holographic display showing a star chart and mysterious symbols.

The 24 Elders

Realm of the Elders:

An otherworldly, serene environment with a celestial ambiance. A vast, ethereal realm filled with glowing orbs and flowing energy streams. The 24 Elders, ancient and wise beings, are seated in a circle, each with a unique aura. The realm glows with a transcendent light. The Elders radiate wisdom and power, their auras shifting colors harmoniously. Seated in a circle, their auras shimmering with energy streams flowing around them, creating harmonious, melodic sounds that resonates with ancient souls.

Elder Akachi: "The mortals are close and are on the brink of unlocking the 12th dimension and uncovering the secrets kept from them for light years. They have made a significant discovery, but I am not sure they are ready. We must guide them carefully."

24: Universal Economics and the Song of the Elders

Elder Zamarachi: "Their intentions are noble, sometimes, but their understanding is limited. I mean their understanding is growing, but they must be guided…it's a must. They take everything as a game—The 'Song' they seek is more than a key; it is a binding force of the multiverse."

Elder Amadiahia: "If they misuse it, they could unravel the fabric of reality. We must ensure they are prepared…or destroy their efforts and trap them in chains of darkness…again."

Elder Akachi: "We will send them a guide. One who understands both their world and ours, someone that looks like them, but who carries our light— someone they are not threatened by…One who can bridge the gap."

Elder Amadiahia: "But if they misuse this knowledge. The entire balance of the multiverse is at stake."

The Elders begin to chant softly, and a beam of light emerges from the center of their circle, heading towards Earth. The Song of the 24 Elders fills the air, resonating with the very fabric of the multiverse.

The Realm of Fate

24: Universal Economics and the Song of the Elders

Aka Ra Aka:

A surreal landscape with floating threads of light, representing the delicate balance of fate. The air hums with a mystical energy, and **Ala--the Woman Clothed with the Sun** stands as a majestic figure. Aka Ra Aka, is a mysterious and mystical realm where fate is woven. The environment is surreal, with shimmering threads of destiny floating in the air creating a tapestry of possibilities. Lila finds herself in a surreal landscape, with threads of light floating around her, representing the delicate balance of fate. The Woman Clothed with the Sun stands before her, a majestic figure with an aura of power.

Lila: "Where am I? What is this place?"

Ala: "You are in Aka Ra Aka, the realm where fate is decided. I am the guardian of this realm."

Lila: "Why was I brought here?"

Addida (Fate Weaver): "You have been chosen to witness the power of fate. Your journey will intertwine with the destiny of the 12 dimensions."

Ala: "The vision you saw, 'the women are heads and the heads are women,' symbolizes the interconnectedness of all beings. Your role is crucial."

Lila looks around, mesmerized by the floating threads and the sense of immense power.

The Call

Mountain Cabin:

𝓐 remote, rustic, tranquil cabin in the Appalachian Mountains, Arkansas, USA. The setting is surrounded by nature. The porch is illuminated by the soft glow of the stars and the night sky is vast and clear., providing a sense of peace and isolation., where Dr. Tanis retreats for contemplation.

Dr. Tanis sits on the porch, staring at the stars, lost in thought.

The Call: "Alara..."

Dr. Tanis: *startled* "Who... Who's there?"

The Call: "You have been chosen to uncover the mysteries of the 12th dimension. The Elders have sent a guide."

24: Universal Economics and the Song of the Elders

Dr. Tanis: "A guide? What do you mean?"

The Call: "Listen to the Song of the 24 Elders. Trust in the process. You are not alone."

The voice fades, and Dr. Tanis feels a shiver up her spine which could not begin to describe the shock she was in, but she also had a quiet, undetectable smile amidst her shock. She felt an urgency to share her encounter with the rest of her team.

The Call: "Amina…"

Enugu, Nigeria

Priestess Amina's Childhood:

Amina grows up in a small village in Enugu, surrounded by lush greenery and vibrant traditions. She is raised in a family with deep spiritual roots. Amina, as a young girl, attends a traditional ceremony with her grandmother.

Grandmother: "Amina, always remember the spirits of our ancestors guide us. They are in the wind, the trees, and the earth."

Amina: "I feel them, Nne. I feel their presence in everything. These voices in Nkwa (the wind)

24: Universal Economics and the Song of the Elders

Calling: Listen to the Song of the 24 Elders. Trust in the process. You are not alone."

The quantum links are discovered, the Elders reveal their role as custodians, and the realm of fate--Aka Ra Aka, is introduced. Dr. Alara Tanis and Amina receive a mysterious call, setting the stage for her journey into the unknown. The interconnectedness of the different regions on Earth is highlighted and their roles in the unfolding events, blending modern-day scenarios with ancient mysticism.

The Awakening

Nairobi, Kenya

Nyah Kimani's Childhood:

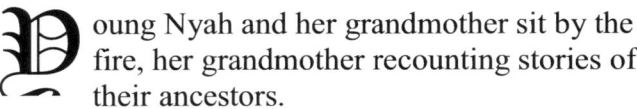oung Nyah and her grandmother sit by the fire, her grandmother recounting stories of their ancestors.

Grandmother (in Kikuyu): "Nyah, maithe maitũ gũkũoya atũ. Itikũrwo ni thayũ, mũingi na gũkũyo. Nĩathurite nĩtigathimĩrie."

Translation: "Nyah, our ancestors have always guided us. They speak through the wind, the

24: Universal Economics and the Song of the Elders

animals, and the earth itself. They watch over us without fail."

Nyah: "Guka, what are the spirits like? Do they protect us always?"

Translation: "Grandma, how are the spirits? Are they always there to protect us?"

Grandmother: "Eh, mwana wa thii. Miaka ya mirimu, itikũrwo na athamaki. Inĩona kĩhoro mũrata na inĩoneire mũrimu. Nĩmaithe matũ, maũkĩrĩe arume ta athũ ĩtara na mathaitha."

Translation: "Ah, my child. The spirits are both gentle and fierce. They guide us in times of need and celebrate with us in times of joy. They are our ancestors, watching over us from the hills and valleys."

Nyah: "Nataka kuwa kama wao, Bibi. Nguvu na hekima, kulinda ardhi yetu na watu wetu."

Translation: "I want to be like them, Grandma. Strong and wise, protecting our land and our people."

Grandmother: "Mundũ aũka ũrĩa warĩ na maithe matũ mwiri, Nyah. Mũrata wĩa ũrĩa wa gũcokera aũkĩndire ta mathaitha. Wĩnyitũ na kĩhere."

Translation: "You already have their spirit within you, Nyah. You will grow to be a great leader, guiding our people with your heart and mind."

The High-Tech Laboratory in Switzerland

The Laboratory and Its Operations

The lab is a marvel of modern engineering, a sprawling complex with state-of-the-art facilities nestled in the picturesque countryside of Southeast Switzerland. It is a place where the boundaries of science are continually pushed, and where the mysteries of the universe are explored. The laboratory is surrounded by exuberant rolling hills and pristine lakes, reflecting the natural beauty of Switzerland. The laboratory, funded by a consortium of international bodies including the European Union, private tech firms, and global academic institutions, is a hub of innovation. Its facilities include a particle accelerator, quantum computing labs, and advanced simulation rooms. The sheer scale of the operations requires significant energy, much like CERN, and funding is a constant challenge.

Dr. Tanis: "The collider is ready for the next round of tests. We need to ensure all systems are optimized for maximum efficiency."

24: Universal Economics and the Song of the Elders

Dr. Bern: "Agreed. We've managed to secure additional funding from the EU, but we need to show significant progress to maintain our sponsors' confidence."

Anya Müller: "I'll run diagnostics on the quantum stabilizers. We've had some fluctuations that need addressing before the main test."

The team disperses, each heading to their respective tasks. The laboratory hums with activity, a testament to the brilliance, ingenuity and collaborative effort of its teams.

Social Life in Switzerland

A local juice bar in Zurich, a bustling hub of culture and diversity serving a vast array of freshly juiced exotic fruits.

Dr. Tanis, Dr. Bern, and Anya meet at the local juice bar after a long day in the lab.

Chisom: "The usual for you all?"

Dr. Tanis: "Yes, please. We need all that good energy!"

24: Universal Economics and the Song of the Elders

Marc: "You scientists are always so busy. How's the universe treating you today?"

Dr. Bern: "It's been a challenging day, but we're making progress. We might be on the verge of something groundbreaking."

Anya: "I just hope we don't blow the place up!"

They laugh, appreciating the moment of levity. The juice bar is filled with a mix of locals and expats, reflecting the diverse and vibrant culture of Zurich.

Video Conference with Dr. Mei Wang

Dr. Mei Wang's home in Southeast China. The room is modest but filled with warmth, decorated with traditional Chinese art highlighting the personal side of a dedicated scientist.

Dr. Mei Wang prepares for the video conference while trying to manage her playful niece.

Dr. Mei Wang: "Wǒ de bǎobèi, zhùshǒu chūlái!" (我的宝贝，住手出来！ - My darling, stop that now!)

Niece: "Lái zhǎo wǒ ba!" (来找我吧！ - Come and get me!)

Tai-Zamarai Yasharahyalah | 35

24: Universal Economics and the Song of the Elders

The niece giggles as she rides the family cat around the room. The video call connects, and the other participants can't help but chuckle at the scene.

Dr. Tanis: "I see you've got your hands full. Is this a bad time? As you are aware, this is of huge importance. I will be more than happy to reschedule this meeting."

Dr. Mei Wang: "Tíngxià, wǒ bù kāiwánxiào!" (停下，我不开玩笑！- Stop now, I am not kidding…)

She turns to the group.

Dr. Mei Wang: "Pardon me, you will have my undivided attention in a moment. This meeting cannot wait, but so does life!"

Dr. Bern: "Take your time, Mei. We understand."

Dr. Wang finally manages to settle her niece and focuses on the screen.

Dr. Mei Wang: "Alright, let's proceed. We have important developments to discuss regarding the stabilization algorithms."

The meeting continues, with each participant fully engaged in the critical discussion. Despite the initial chaos, the team know they need to squeeze the most out of every opportune meeting.

24: *Universal Economics and the Song of the Elders*

Song | 2

Awakening

12 Realities, 12 Possibilities

The Second Song in Southeastern China

Dr. Mei Wang shares the song with local scholars.

Her niece, fascinated, starts to mimic the song's melody.

The scholars begin to suspect the song has spiritual significance.

Mei: "This song—it feels ancient, like it carries the weight of millennia."

Scholar 1: "These symbols resemble old Chinese script, but they are far more intricate."

Scholar 2: "There's a spiritual essence to it. Could it be a message from the heavens?"

24: Universal Economics and the Song of the Elders

SONG 2

24: Universal Economics and the Song of the Elders

Transliteration

<u>Ahrahyah</u>

Mmiri di awcha na-asawpiwta n'imai mmiri miri aimi.

Ailiwigwai na mbara igwai na-aiziwtai n'aibai di anya.

Iphiwphai Chi-na-Aka na-aiphaiphai n'aibai niilai.

Na-aigyi nwayaw aimai ka awa di awhiwriw.

Igbo Translation

<u>Orie</u>

Ubọchị ahịa Orie mbụ

Mmiri dị ọcha na-asọpụta n'ime mmiri miri emi.

Eluigwe na mbara igwe na-ezute n'ebe dị anya.

Ifufe Chineke na-efefe n'ebe niile.

Na-eji nwayọ eme ka ụwa dị ọhụrụ.

24: Universal Economics and the Song of the Elders

English Translation:

Ahrayah

First Ahrayah Market Rise

Pure waters flow in deep currents,

Heaven and sky meet at a distant horizon.

Divine wind blows through all,

Renewing the world with a gentle touch.

Origins and Responsibilities

Ancestral Archives of the Elders

The Ancestral Archives of the Elders is a vast hall filled with towering shelves of ancient tomes, glowing scrolls, and crystalline records that float gently in the air. The walls are adorned with murals depicting the history of the multiverse and the ascension of the Elders. The air is filled with a hum of energy, a tangible presence of the wisdom stored within these sacred halls. At the centre of the Archives is a grand, circular table made of polished ebony wood, inlaid with silver runes that pulse with a gentle light. This is where the Elders gather to delve into their past, reflect on

24: Universal Economics and the Song of the Elders

their duties, and discuss the ongoing challenges they face.

Description of the Elders' Origins and Responsibilities

Elder Mmbagwiw, the Keeper of Light:

- *Origin:* Mmbagwiw was a being of pure light, born from the first dawn of the multiverse. Her wisdom and purity made her a natural leader among the realms of light.

- *Responsibilities*: Mmbagwiw oversees all matters of illumination and enlightenment. She ensures that the light of knowledge and truth permeates throughout the dimensions, guiding beings towards higher understanding and harmony.

Elder Zaphyr Nkwa, the Master of Winds:

- *Origin:* Nkwa emerged from the first breath of the cosmic winds, embodying freedom and change. His presence brought balance to the ever-shifting air currents of the multiverse.

- *Responsibilities:* Nkwa controls the winds and air currents, ensuring they flow smoothly and bring balance to the elements. He also aids in communication and the spread of messages across realms.

Elder Zaphyr Nnshimiri, the Guardian of Oceans:

- *Origin:* Nnshimiri was born from the primordial seas, embodying the depths and mysteries of the waters. Her serene nature and deep understanding of the oceans made her the perfect guardian.

- *Responsibilities:* Thalassa governs all bodies of water, from the smallest streams to the vast oceans. She maintains the balance of aquatic life and ensures the purity and flow of water throughout the realms.

Elder Abaraka the Wielder of Flames:

- *Origin:* Abaraka commonly known as Aka, arose from the first spark of creation, representing the energy and transformative power of fire. His fiery spirit and strength made him a formidable leader.

- *Responsibilities:* Ignis oversees all aspects of fire, from warmth and light to destruction and rebirth. He ensures that fire is used wisely and that its power is harnessed for growth and renewal.

24: Universal Economics and the Song of the Elders

The Elders gather around the grand table, their expressions a mix of contemplation and determination.

Elder Mmbagwiw: (softly glowing) "Our origins tie us to our responsibilities, and it is these origins that give us the strength to face the challenges before us. Yet, the weight of our duties grows heavier with each passing eon."

Elder Nkwa: (voice like a gentle breeze) "Indeed, the winds whisper of unrest in the realms of air. There are those who seek to disrupt the natural order, creating storms of chaos and discord."

Elder Nnshimiri: (calm and flowing) "The oceans, too, are not immune to these disturbances. I sense a growing imbalance in the depths, a restlessness that threatens to spill over into the surface realms."

Elder Abaraka: (fiery and intense) "The flames burn hotter and wilder. There are those who would misuse the power of fire, turning it into a force of destruction rather than a tool for renewal."

Elder Saraphina: (ethereal and serene) "We must remember our origins and the responsibilities they bestowed upon us. It is through our connection to these primordial forces that we can restore balance."

Elder Achichi: (strength and determination) "Our roles are not just about governance but about protection and guidance. We must find a way to address these disturbances before they escalate further."

Elder Mmbagwiw: "Our first step must be understanding the source of these disruptions. Only then can we formulate a plan to restore harmony."

Elder Nkwa: "I will call upon the spirits of the winds to gather information. Their whispers will guide us to the root of the chaos."

Elder Nnshimiri "I will consult with the ancient beings of the deep. Their wisdom and insight may reveal the hidden causes of the turmoil."

Elder Abaraka: "I will focus on those who wield fire. It is crucial to ensure that its power is used for creation and not for destruction."

Elder Saraphina: "And I will meditate on the cosmic energies, seeking clarity and guidance from the higher realms."

Elder Achichi: "Together, we will face these challenges as we always have. Our unity and combined wisdom are our greatest strengths."

As the Elders disperse to their respective tasks, the air in the Ancestral Archives hums with renewed purpose. Each Elder is reminded of their origins and responsibilities, drawing strength from their unique connections to the fundamental forces of the multiverse. Their combined efforts will be crucial in addressing the disturbances and restoring the balance that ensures the harmony of all realms.

The Integration Chamber

A futuristic facility hidden deep within the Swiss Alps. The chamber is a large, circular room with advanced technology lining the walls. The air hums with the energy of the machinery.

Dr. Tanis and Dr. Dubois stand by the control panel, while Ida prepares the equipment. The room is filled with a low, steady hum.

Dr. Tanis: "This is the Integration Chamber. It's designed to synchronize our consciousness with the quantum links we've discovered."

Dr. Dubois: "If successful, this will allow us to perceive and interact with the 12th dimension."

Ida: "Everything's set. Ready to initiate the sequence?"

Dr. Tanis: "Let's begin. Ida, activate the synchronizers."

Ida presses a series of buttons, and the chamber comes to life. Lights pulse rhythmically, and the hum grows louder. Dr. Tanis and Dr. Dubois close their eyes, focusing on the process.

Separated by Fate

Aka Ra Aka, --the Realm of Fate.

Lila is standing among the threads of destiny, feeling their pull. She walks through the threads of destiny, each one tugging at her with different emotions and memories.

Lila: "I can feel so many lives, so many possibilities. It's overwhelming."

Ala: "Each thread represents a different reality, a different path. You must find the one that aligns with your destiny."

Addida: "Your fate is intertwined with the 12 dimensions. To find your true path, you must understand the power of these threads."

Lila: "Here goes everything!"

Lila: reaches out to a thread that glows brighter than the others. As she touches it, a vision of a different reality floods her mind.

The Impossible Recall

A quiet holistic café in Peckham, London with a warm ambiance serving all things natural. The modern setting contrasts with the surreal experiences of Zam Zam, creating a sense of normalcy amidst the extraordinary.

Zam Zam sits at a table, staring into his naturally sweetened hot chocolate. Amma joins him, concerned.

Amma: "Zam, you've been so distant lately. What's going on?"

Zam Zam: "It's hard to explain. I feel like I've seen things, been places I can't remember. it's either that or my mind is fried."

Amma: "What do you mean?"

Mysterious Stranger: *appearing suddenly* "The memories of your journey to the 12th dimension is suppressed, but not gone. You have to unlock them."

Zam Zam: "Who are you?"

Mysterious Stranger: "A guide. The Elders sent me to help you recall your experiences. There is a chance to remember, but it won't be easy."

24: Universal Economics and the Song of the Elders

Zam Zam looks at the stranger, torn between skepticism and a deep-seated belief.

Zam Zam: What's the worst that can happen, I already feel like I am losing my mind. Sure! What do I have to do?"

One More Chance

A bustling market in Enugu, Nigeria. The vibrant colors and sounds of the market create a lively atmosphere. The market is a hub of activity, showcasing the rich culture and traditions of Nigeria. Chimamanda browses through the market stalls, drawn to Trader Kofi's exotic goods.

Chimamanda: "These items... they feel familiar, but I don't know why."

Trader Kofi: "You sense their power. They are from other realms, connected to your destiny."

High Priestess Amina: *approaching* "Chimamanda, you have been given another chance. Your path intersects with the 12 dimensions."

Chimamanda: "Another chance? What do you mean?"

24: Universal Economics and the Song of the Elders

High Priestess Amina: "Your fate was disrupted, but you can still fulfill your destiny. Trust in the process and in yourself."

Chimamanda takes a deep breath, feeling a renewed sense of purpose.

The characters are beginning to explore the practical implications of the quantum links and their connection to the 12th dimension. Dr. Tanis and her team attempt to synchronize their consciousness with the quantum links in the Integration Chamber. Lila navigates the realm of fate, Aka Ra Aka, and learns about the threads of destiny. Zam Zam struggles with suppressed memories of his journey and is told he will receive guidance to unlock them. Chimamanda in Enugu is given another chance to fulfill her destiny, highlighting the theme of redemption and second chances. We see the emotional and psychological struggles of the characters as they come to terms with their roles in the unfolding events.

24: Universal Economics and the Song of the Elders

Song | 3

The Mechanics of Creation

The Third Song in Nigeria

Priestess Amina's Temple

Priestess Amina receives the third song in a vision. She gathers her initiates to interpret the song's meaning. The village elders join to provide insights based on their ancient traditions.

Amina: "This song is a gift from the heavens. It holds the key to our future."

Initiate 1: "The symbols are similar to those in our ancient texts. What do they mean, Priestess?"

Elder: "These songs might be guiding us to restore balance. We must heed their wisdom."

24: Universal Economics and the Song of the Elders

Tai-Zamarai Yasharahyalah | 52

24: Universal Economics and the Song of the Elders

Transliteration

Ahphar

Ala na-aimai nri na-ainyai ndiw,

Mkpiwriw na-aipiwlitai na ngawzi nkai chi gbiwbaw awhiwriw.

A na-abiw abiw awlilaianya n'idi n'awtiw.

Awgbiwgba ndiw nkai ihai na ihiwnanya na-ainwaighi awkai.

Igbo Translation

Afọ

ụbọchị ahịa Afọ mbụ

Ala na-eme nri na-enye ndụ,

Mkpụrụ na-epulite na ngọzi nke chi ọbụbọ ọhụrụ.

A na-abụ abụ olileanya n'ịdị n'otu.

Ọgbụgba ndụ nke ihè na ịhụnanya na-enweghị oke.

24: Universal Economics and the Song of the Elders

English Translation:

Ahphar

First Ahphar Market Rise

Fertile earth bestows life,

Seeds sprout in the blessing of a new dawn.

Songs of hope are sung in unity,

A covenant of boundless light and love.

Council Meetings and Decisions

The Great Hall of Justice

The Great Hall of Justice is a majestic, awe-inspiring chamber. Its vaulted ceilings are adorned with intricate frescoes depicting the cosmic balance and the eternal struggle between order and chaos. The hall's walls are lined with towering columns made of shimmering, translucent crystal, reflecting the light in a spectrum of colors. At the centre of the hall is a circular dais with 24 thrones, each uniquely designed to represent the individual Elder who occupies it. The atmosphere is solemn and charged with anticipation as the Elders prepare to convene for one of their most crucial meetings. The fate of the 12 realms hangs in the

24: Universal Economics and the Song of the Elders

balance, and the weight of their responsibility is palpable.

The Decision-Making Processes and Conflicts of Interest

As the Elders take their seats, the air hums with a mix of tension and determination. Each Elder brings their own unique perspective, shaped by their origins and the realms they govern. The council meetings are a blend of rigorous debate, strategic thinking, and deep reflection, as they strive to reach decisions that will uphold the balance and harmony of the multiverse.

Elder Mmbagwiw: (radiant and calm) "Shi-Ala-M Ahia-Ala Kan."

Elders Respond (in Unison): "Wa Ahia Ala Kan Shi-Ala-M"

Elder Mmbagwiw: "Welcome, esteemed Elders. This rise, we face a matter of grave importance. The balance of the 12 realms is being threatened by forces of chaos and discord. We must decide on the best course of action to restore harmony."

Elder Nkwa: (voice like a gentle breeze) "The winds have carried whispers of unrest. There are factions within the realms of air that seek to disrupt

24: Universal Economics and the Song of the Elders

the natural order. We must act swiftly to quell these disturbances."

Elder Nnshimiri: (serene and flowing) "The oceans too are in turmoil. I sense a growing imbalance in the depths, a restlessness that threatens to spill over into the surface realms. We must address the root causes of this disturbance."

Elder Abaraka: (fiery and intense) "The flames burn hotter and wilder. There are those who would misuse the power of fire, turning it into a force of destruction rather than a tool for renewal. We must ensure that fire is used wisely."

Elder Saraphina: (ethereal and serene) "Too late for that!" She Murmurs, "I mean, we must meditate on the cosmic energies and seek guidance from the higher realms. Only then can we find the clarity needed to make the right decisions."

Elder Achichi: (strength and determination) "The darkness carries with it a division that is spreading rapidly into all realms. We must act decisively and with Unity, or we risk spiralling into chaos like these foolish mortals. We are light, and light cannot be threathned by darkness. Our combined wisdom and strength are our greatest assets. We cannot afford to be divided in the face of these challenges."

Elder Amadiahia: (stern and resolute) "I propose we deploy our forces to the most affected areas and restore order through strength. We must show that we will not tolerate any disruptions to the balance of the realms."

Tazadaaka: (peaceful and diplomatic) "While strength is necessary, we must also seek to understand the underlying causes of the unrest. Dialogue and diplomacy should be our first course of action."

Elder Mmgbar: (perfect and precise) "Dialogue and Diplomacy. Elder Mmgbar scoffs, "With whom, mortals? To what end. We all know time is a fundamental factor that cannot be understated…and here you are speaking of diplomacy!"

Elder Achichi: (strength and determination) "This is exactly my point; we cannot afford to be divided at all…but here we…no seed of discord must germinate amonst us. We resolve any and all challenges with one resolve. One!"

Elder Amaka: (grounded and nurturing) "The natural order must be respected. We should work to heal the land and waters, restoring the balance through nurturing and care."

Elder Amachichiri: (mysterious and contemplative) "The stars have foretold this upheaval. We must study the cosmic alignments and prepare for the challenges that lie ahead. Our decisions must be informed by the wisdom of the stars."

24: Universal Economics and the Song of the Elders

Elder Amamihia: (brilliant and commanding) "Our primary goal is to restore harmony. We must be strategic in our approach, balancing strength with wisdom, and ensuring that our actions lead to lasting peace."

Elder Mmbagwiw: (calm and reflective) "The moon's cycles remind us that balance is a delicate dance. We must be patient and deliberate in our decisions, considering all perspectives before taking action."

Elder Mmgbar: (perfect and precise) "I hear that, but not too patient!"

All the Elders laugh hysterically, as they share a moment of Mmgbar's humour that sharply cuts through the tension in the air. As the debate continues, the Elders present their arguments, each rooted in their unique perspectives and the realms they govern. The hall resonates with their voices, a symphony of wisdom, passion, and conviction.

Elder Mmbagwiw: "We have heard many wise and compelling arguments. Let us now move towards a decision. We must balance strength with wisdom, action with reflection. Only then can we restore harmony to the 12 realms."

Elder Nkwa: "I propose we form a task force, composed of representatives from each realm, to

Tai-Zamarai Yasharahyalah | 58

address the immediate threats while we continue to seek long-term solutions through diplomacy and healing."

Elder Nnshimiri: "I agree. This task force should also include healers and diplomats, to address the underlying causes of the unrest and work towards lasting peace."

Elder Alara: Undercover perhaps?

Elder Abaraka: "Given the current state of the mindset of these mortals, definitely. We must ensure that our forces are prepared for any eventuality. The flames of war must not be ignited, but we must be ready to defend the balance if necessary."

Elder Saraphina: "And we must continue to seek guidance from the higher realms, meditating on the cosmic energies and aligning our actions with the greater good."

With a collective nod, the Elders reach a consensus. A task force will be formed, composed of representatives from each realm, to address the immediate threats while also working towards long-term solutions through diplomacy, healing, and strategic action. The decision is made, and the

24: Universal Economics and the Song of the Elders

Elders rise from their seats, united in their resolve to restore harmony to the multiverse.

The Great Hall of Justice, once filled with tension, now hums with a collective voice and a renewed sense of purpose and determination.

Universal Oversights

Conference Room in Geneva:

A sleek, high-tech room with holographic displays and advanced technology. The atmosphere is one of intense focus and intellectual collaboration.

The team is gathered around a large table with a holographic display in the center, showing complex diagrams of the multiverse.

Dr. Tanis: "Our initial exploration of the 12th dimension has revealed significant gaps in our understanding. We need to address these universal oversights."

Dr. Dubois: "Agreed. The data suggests there are mechanisms at play beyond our current models."

Dr. Wang: *via video call* "In Beijing, we've observed anomalies that indicate a higher order of organization. We need to decode these patterns."

24: Universal Economics and the Song of the Elders

Professor Petrova: "It's not just about understanding; it's about integration. Our models must evolve to accommodate these new realities."

Ida "What if the key lies in the ancient texts? The Song of the 24 Elders might hold clues to these mechanisms."

The team nods in agreement, preparing to delve deeper into the ancient wisdom and its connection to modern science.

The Process of Purchasing Universal Sovereignty

A majestic hall in Kinshasa, Democratic Republic of the Congo decorated with symbols representing the 12 dimensions. The setting is grand and formal, emphasizing the importance of the assembly's work. The delegates are seated around a large circular table. President Lumumba stands at the centre, addressing the assembly.

President Lumumba: "The process of purchasing universal sovereignty is complex and requires a unified approach. We must establish clear guidelines."

Delegate from Switzerland: "How do we ensure fair distribution of resources across dimensions?"

24: Universal Economics and the Song of the Elders

Chimamanda: "By recognizing the interconnectedness of our realms. Each dimension contributes uniquely to the universal economy."

Delegate from China: "We need a regulatory framework that balances power and responsibility."

President Lumumba: "Agreed. Let's draft a charter that outlines these principles and ensures equitable governance."

The delegates begin drafting the Universal Charter, a document that will guide the governance of the 12 dimensions.

Universal Economy

A futuristic marketplace in Southeast Honduras. The vibrant, bustling market is filled with colorful stalls and traders from different dimensions exchanging exotic goods. The atmosphere is lively and energetic. Trader Kofi stands behind his stall, showcasing a variety of goods from different dimensions. The market is alive with activity.

Local Buyer: "These items are extraordinary. How do you obtain them?"

24: Universal Economics and the Song of the Elders

Trader Kofi: "Through interstellar transactions. The universal economy is based on the exchange of rare and valuable resources from different realms."

High Priestess Amina: *approaching* "The balance of the universal economy is crucial. Each transaction affects the stability of our interconnected realms."

Local Buyer: "How can we ensure fair trade?"

Trader Kofi: "By adhering to the principles set forth in the Universal Charter. Trust and fairness are the foundation of our economy."

The buyer nods, understanding the importance of maintaining balance in the universal economy.

Delving into the deeper mechanics of the universe and the creation process, the team in Geneva identifies significant gaps in their understanding and resolves to decode the ancient wisdom of the Song of the 24 Elders. In Kinshasa, the assembly discusses the process of purchasing universal sovereignty and begins drafting the Universal Charter to ensure fair governance. The bustling marketplace in Honduras highlights the complexities of the universal economy and the importance of fair trade. There is an intricate balance required to maintain harmony across the

12 dimensions and collaborative efforts are needed to achieve it.

Amina's Call to Action

Priestess Amina's Temple

Amina calls for a gathering to discuss the impending crisis. She rallies her initiates and the village to take action. They prepare rituals to communicate with the Elders.

Amina: "The balance of our world is in jeopardy. We must act now."

Initiate 1: "We are ready, Priestess. What must we do?"

Amina: "We will perform the ancient rituals to reach the Elders and seek their guidance."

24: Universal Economics and the Song of the Elders

The Integration Chamber, the Heart of the 12th Dimension

The Integration Chamber is a grand hall in the heart of the 12th dimension, a place where universal laws are conceived and executed. The chamber is filled with glowing symbols and floating holograms that constantly shift, representing the ever-changing nature of the multiverse. The Integration Chamber is abuzz with activity. Elders Amadiahia and Elder Achichi are in deep discussion, surrounded by holographic displays showing different realms and timelines.

Elder Amadiahia: "The recent anomalies in the Aka Ra Aka realm are troubling. We must ensure that the balance is restored."

Elder Achichi: "Indeed. The ripples are affecting the quantum links to other realms. We need to reassess our strategies."

Cosmic Observers: "Elders, we've detected an unusual surge of energy in the Earth dimension. It appears to be originating from multiple points simultaneously."

Elder Amadiahia: "This could be the result of the intergalactic transactions we've been observing. We must investigate further."

24: Universal Economics and the Song of the Elders

Elder Achichi: "Agreed. Dispatch the Universal intermediaries to Earth. We need to understand the source of this energy and its implications."

The Laboratory in Switzerland

The high-tech laboratory in back in Switzerland continues to play a crucial role in the unfolding events. The laboratory is bustling with excitement as the team prepares for a significant experiment.

Dr. Tanis: "We've calibrated the collider to the new specifications. This should allow us to tap into the energy fluctuations we've been monitoring."

Dr. Bern: "Let's proceed with caution. The last thing we need is an overload."

Anya Müller: "All systems are green. Ready when you are."

Dr. Tanis: "Initiate the sequence."

The laboratory lights dim as the collider powers up. The screens show a surge of energy, and the team watches intently as the data streams in.

24: Universal Economics and the Song of the Elders

Dr. Bern: "Look at that! The energy readings are off the charts!"

Dr. Tanis: "This could be the breakthrough we've been waiting for. Let's compile the data and prepare for the next phase."

Life in Southeast China

Dr. Mei Wang's home and surroundings in Southeast China. Dr. Mei Wang sits at her desk, reviewing the data from the Swiss lab, while her niece plays nearby.

Dr. Mei Wang's Niece: "Gūgu, wǒ kěyǐ kàn nǐ de diànnǎo ma?" (姑姑，我可以看你的电脑吗？ - Auntie, can I see your computer?)

Dr. Mei Wang: "Bù xíng, wǒ zhèng zài gōngzuò. Nǐ yīnggāi qù wán qítā de dōngxī." (不行，我正在工作。你应该去玩其他的东西。 - No, I'm working. You should go play with something else.)

Her niece pouts but then runs off to play outside. Dr. Wang smiles, then joins a video call with the Swiss team.

24: Universal Economics and the Song of the Elders

Dr. Tanis: "Mei, the latest results are promising. We need your input on the energy dispersal patterns."

Dr. Mei Wang: "Of course. I'll run simulations on my end and share the findings. Let's ensure we maintain stability across all phases."

Dr. Bern: "We appreciate your support, Mei. Your insights are invaluable."

After the call, Dr. Wang steps outside, taking a deep breath of the fresh mountain air. She exchanges greetings with local villagers as she walks to the market.

Dr. Mei Wang: "Nǐmen hǎo, jīntiān zěnme yàng?" (你们好，今天怎么样？ - Hello, how are you today?)

Villager 1: "Hěn hǎo, xièxiè. Nǐ ne?" (很好，谢谢。你呢？ - Very well, thank you. And you?)**Dr. Mei Wang:** "Wǒ yě hěn hǎo. Gōngzuò hěn máng, dànshì hěn jìnzhǎn." (我也很好。工作很忙，但是很进展。 - I'm also very well. Work is busy but progressing well.)

24: Universal Economics and the Song of the Elders

An Initiate's Story in Kenya

Mwende's village in Southeast Kenya, amidst preparations for her journey. Mwende sits with her mother, who is weaving a basket under the shade of an acacia tree.

Mwende: "Mama, nina ndoto nyingi kuhusu safari hii. Naogopa lakini nina matumaini." (Mama, I have many dreams about this journey. I am scared but hopeful.)

Mama Mwende: "Usijali, Mwende. Ndoto zako ni sehemu ya safari yako. Utajifunza mengi na kurudi nyumbani kwa heshima." (Don't worry, Mwende. Your dreams are part of your journey. You will learn much and return home with honor.)

Kijana approaches, carrying a small satchel.

Kijana: "Mwende, hizi ni zawadi kutoka kwa wazee wa kijiji. Zinakuhusu nguvu na ulinzi katika safari yako." (Mwende, these are gifts from the village elders. They will give you strength and protection on your journey.)

Mwende: "Asante sana, Kijana. Nitahifadhi maneno yako moyoni na kutumia zawadi hizi kwa hekima." (Thank you very much, Kijana. I will keep your words in my heart and use these gifts wisely.)

24: Universal Economics and the Song of the Elders

Kijana places a hand on Mwende's shoulder, offering a blessing.

Kijana: "Mwende, safiri salama. Wazee na mababu wapo nawe." (Mwende, travel safely. The elders and ancestors are with you.)

Mwende looks at the horizon, feeling a mixture of fear and excitement about the journey ahead.

Exploration into the intricate mechanics of the universe and creation continues, with a focus on the Integration Chamber in the 12th dimension. Elders Amadiahia and Achichi discuss the challenges of maintaining balance across the multiverse, highlighting the interconnectedness of different realms. On Earth, the Swiss laboratory team, including Dr. Mei Wang in China, make significant progress in their experiments, showing the collaborative effort in scientific discovery. The personal lives of the characters are also portrayed, showcasing the rich cultural backgrounds of Nigeria and Kenya, and universal and earthly dimensions. Emphasizing the importance of balance and harmony in the grand scheme of creation.

Song | 4

Love at First Flight

The Forth Song in Kenya

Kenyan village, sacred forest

- A Kenyan initiate receives the song during a ritual in the sacred forest.

- Local shamans assist in deciphering the song, connecting it to their spiritual practices.

- A sense of urgency emerges as they realize the song's implications for the world.

Initiate: "This song feels like a warning. It speaks to the heart of the earth."

Shaman 1: "The symbols align with our ancient markings. We must understand its message."

Shaman 2: "It's a call to action. The balance of the world is at stake."

24: Universal Economics and the Song of the Elders

Ibar (Ancient Paleo- Hebrew/ Phoenician Script

SONG 4

24: Universal Economics and the Song of the Elders

Transliteration

Nkwa

Awkiw nkai akaka na-aigyi awbi ikai na-airai awkiw,

A na-akpiwzi awa n'imai ikiwkiw nkai idi adi.

Awbi ndi Di ikai na-aidiwzi iwzaw.

Na-achaw aiziawkwiw kariri mbara igwai.

Igbo Translation

NKwọ

ụbọchị ahịa Nkwọ mbụ

Ọkụ nke okike na-eji obi ike na-ere ọkụ,

A na-akpụzi ụwa n'ime ikuku nke ịdị adị.

Obi ndị dị ike na-eduzi ụzọ.

Na-achọ eziokwu karịrị mbara igwe.

24: Universal Economics and the Song of the Elders

English Translation:

Nkwa

First Nkwa Market Rise

Fire of creation burns with courage,

Worlds are shaped in the whirlwind of existence.

Brave hearts guide the way,

Seeking truth beyond the horizon.

Interactions with Higher Beings

Celestial Observatory

The Celestial Observatory is a sanctum of profound wisdom and unearthly beauty. Positioned at the highest point of the 12th Dimension, it offers a panoramic view of the cosmos, with stars and galaxies shimmering in the vast expanse. The observatory is constructed from luminescent materials that glow with an inner light, casting an ethereal radiance across the chamber. At its center lies an intricate orrery, representing the multiverse and its countless dimensions, each orb revolving in a delicate dance.

24: Universal Economics and the Song of the Elders

The Elders gather here to seek counsel from higher-dimensional beings, entities of pure light and wisdom who guide and illuminate their path. The atmosphere is serene and charged with a sense of reverence as the Elders prepare for this sacred communion.

As the Elders stand in a circle around the orrery, they close their eyes in unison, entering a state of deep meditation. The air around them shimmers, and slowly, radiant beings of light begin to materialize within the observatory. These celestial entities, known as the Luminaries, emanate an aura of infinite wisdom and compassion, their forms ever-shifting and filled with vibrant colors.

The Elders open their eyes, gazing with awe and respect at the Luminaries. These interactions are rare and precious, providing insights that transcend the Elders' own innderstanding.

Luminary Awraiahia: (voice resonating like a celestial choir) "Greetings, esteemed Elders. We sense the weight of your burdens and the challenges you face in maintaining the balance of the 12 realms. What wisdom do you seek from us today?"

Elder Alara: (bowing respectfully) "We seek guidance on the current upheavals within the realms. The forces of chaos and discord grow stronger, and we must restore harmony. How can we navigate these turbulent times?"

Luminary Alayasia: (glowing with a soft, soothing light) "The unrest you witness is a reflection of the evolving consciousness within your realms. As souls ascend and grow, they encounter resistance. This is a natural part of the cosmic dance. You must nurture this growth while mitigating the chaos it brings."

Elder Nkwa: (thoughtful) "How do we strike this balance? Our actions must be both firm and compassionate, but the path is unclear."

Luminary Saraphahia: (radiating wisdom) "Trust in the inherent wisdom of the souls you govern. Provide them with the tools and guidance they need to evolve, and they will find their own balance. Encourage unity and understanding among them, for division only breeds more chaos."

Elder Nshimiri: "We have formed a task force to address the immediate threats and work towards long-term solutions. Is this the correct approach?"

Luminary Alahiaigwiwia: (shimmering with brilliance) "Yes, but ensure that this task force is a beacon of hope and unity. It must represent the diversity and strengths of all realms, embodying the harmony you wish to restore."

24: Universal Economics and the Song of the Elders

Elder Achichi: (determined) "We are prepared to defend the balance with strength if necessary. But we wish to avoid conflict if possible."

Luminary Asathiala: (emanating calm) "Strength should be your last resort. Seek first to understand and heal. The use of force, while sometimes necessary, must be tempered with wisdom and compassion. Remember, true power lies in unity and love."

As the conversation continues, the Luminaries share their profound insights, guiding the Elders towards a deeper understanding of the universal laws and the nature of consciousness. They discuss the evolution of souls, emphasizing the importance of nurturing growth and fostering unity across dimensions.

Elder Awraiahia: "The fate of souls is intertwined with the fabric of the multiverse. Each soul's journey contributes to the collective evolution. Encourage self-discovery and enlightenment, for this will lead to a harmonious existence."

Elder Saraphina: (reflective) "How can we better support the evolution of consciousness within our realms?"

Luminary Alayasia: "Create spaces of learning and transformation. Encourage the sharing of

24: Universal Economics and the Song of the Elders

knowledge and experiences. Promote practices that align with the higher vibrations of love and compassion. By doing so, you will raise the collective consciousness."

Elder Abaraka: "And what of those who resist this evolution? How do we guide them without imposing our will?"

Luminary Saraphahia: "Patience and inndderstanding are your greatest allies. Offer guidance without force. Provide opportunities for growth and trust that each soul will find its path in its own time."

With these words, the Luminaries begin to fade, their light gently dissipating into the ether. The Elders remain, their hearts and minds filled with newfound clarity and resolve. They inndderstand that their role is not just to govern, but to guide and nurture the souls within their realms, fostering a collective evolution that transcends the boundaries of the multiverse.

The Celestial Observatory, once again quiet and serene, stands as a testament to the eternal quest for wisdom and harmony.

24: Universal Economics and the Song of the Elders

The Relationship Between Souls

Temple in Southeast China:

A peaceful and spiritual setting surrounded by exultant gardens and ancient stone statues. The temple exudes tranquility and wisdom. Dr. Wang and Yara walk through the temple gardens, accompanied by Liang. The air is filled with the scent of blooming flowers and the sound of a distant waterfall.

Dr. Wang: "Liang, we're trying to understand the connection between souls across the 12 dimensions. How do they interact?"

Liang: "Souls are the essence of life, transcending time and space. They are interconnected through the threads of fate and love."

Yara: "But how do these connections influence our realities?"

Liang: "When souls resonate with each other, they create a harmonious frequency that can alter the fabric of the multiverse. Love is the purest form of this resonance."

Dr. Wang takes notes, inspired by the monk's wisdom, while Yara feels a deep sense of peace and understanding like each word was alive and actively enveloping her in a cloud of wisdom, piercing her like a double edged sword—exposing the thoughts and intent from within

---

Creation of Souls and Soul Inflation

Laboratory in Somerset, UK:

A high-tech lab filled with advanced technology and research equipment. The atmosphere is one of intense focus and innovation. The team is gathered around a large holographic display showing the process of soul creation and inflation. The room is filled with the hum of machinery.

Dr. Dubois: "Our research indicates that souls are created through a process of energy condensation in the 12th dimension."

Ida: "But what about soul inflation? How does that affect the universal economy?"

Professor Petrova: "Soul inflation occurs when the energy balance is disrupted, causing an excess of soul energy. This can lead to instability across the dimensions."

24: Universal Economics and the Song of the Elders

Dr. Tanis: "We need to find a way to stabilize this process. The harmony of the multiverse depends on it."

The team continues to brainstorm, their minds racing with ideas and solutions.

Universal Economic Stability

Conference Room in Arkansas, USA:

A modern room with advanced communication technology and large windows offering a view of a bustling cityscape. The room is filled with charts and data projections. The team is discussing the implications of soul inflation on the universal economy. The room is filled with charts and data projections.

Dr. Tanis: "If we can't control soul inflation, the universal economy could collapse. We need a sustainable solution."

Dr. Dubois: "What if we create a regulatory framework to manage the energy flow between dimensions?"

Ida: "We could use the principles from the Universal Charter to ensure fair distribution and prevent inflation."

Dr. Wang: *via video call* "We must also consider the spiritual aspect. Souls are not just energy; they are connected to the very essence of life."

Ida: "You are absolutely spot on. We need the set regulatory measures prioritised, and enforced rigorously, to prevent the diminishing of cultural expressions, and the homogenisation of generational value systems, which, seems to be the cause of these insane energy spike. My fear is that we might be too late."

The team nods in agreement, realizing the complexity of their task and the importance of balancing both scientific and spiritual elements.

Exploring the deep connection between souls across the 12 dimensions and the impact of love and resonance on the multiverse, Dr. Mei Wang and her team in China delve into the spiritual aspects of soul connections, while the team in Somerset examines the scientific process of soul creation and the challenges of soul inflation. In Arkansas, the team discusses the implications of these findings on the universal economy and the need for a regulatory framework to ensure stability. Highlights are made on the intricate balance between science and spirituality, emphasizing the importance of love and harmony in maintaining the stability of the multiverse.

24: Universal Economics and the Song of the Elders

The Cosmic Plane

The Cosmic Plane is a surreal, ethereal space where souls and higher beings interact. It is a realm of light and energy, with vibrant colors and forms that constantly shift and change. Here, souls are created, relationships are forged, and the universal economy is balanced. In the heart of the Cosmic Plane, Elder Saraphina oversees the creation of new souls. The Soul Architect stands by, ready to begin the intricate process.

Elder Saraphina: "Today, we welcome new souls into the universe. Each soul is a unique embodiment of light and potential."

Elder Saraphina: "Let us begin. The first step is to infuse each soul with the essence of love and purpose."

The Soul Architect gestures, and streams of light converge, forming delicate, shimmering forms. Each young soul pulses with energy, eager to explore the universe.

Elder Saraphina: "Remember, young ones, your journey will be filled with challenges and wonders. Embrace love and compassion in all you do and always be mindful how you affect others."

Young Souls (in unison): "We innderstand, Ahdanah. We are ready."

24: Universal Economics and the Song of the Elders

Love and Relationships

A gathering space within the Cosmic Plane, where souls meet and connect. The Cosmic Plane's gathering space is filled with radiant beings, each representing a different facet of the universe. Souls of all ages and experiences mingle, sharing knowledge and forming bonds.

Elder Saraphina: "Love is the foundation of our existence. It connects us across dimensions and fuels our growth."

Soul Architect: "In this realm, you will experience the purest forms of love. These connections will guide and support you throughout your journeys."

A pair of young souls, drawn to each other by an invisible force, begin to communicate.

Soul 1: "I feel a connection with you, unlike anything I have known before."

Soul 2: "Exactly, you don't know anything, you're just a fresh soul…me…I'm ancient."

Elder Ahdanah: "You, young ones are so funny. Remember, these connections you have with each other are sacred. Nurture them, and they will strengthen you in ways you cannot yet imagine."

24: Universal Economics and the Song of the Elders

Universal Economic Stability

The Cosmic Plane's Council Chamber, where the economy of the universe is managed.

In the Council Chamber, a group of Cosmic Economists discusses the state of the universal economy, ensuring the balance of energy and resources.

Elder Mmbagwiw: "The recent influx of new souls requires careful management of our resources. We must ensure that each realm receives adequate support."

Cosmic Economist: "We have analyzed the energy flows and proposed adjustments to maintain equilibrium. The key is to monitor the soul inflation rate and make necessary corrections."

Elder Saraphina: "Agreed. Our priority is to sustain the harmony of the universe. Let us review the data and implement these changes."

The council members examine the holographic displays, making precise adjustments to the flow of energy and resources across the multiverse.

Cosmic Economist: "These measures will stabilize the universal economy and support the continued growth and development of all realms."

24: Universal Economics and the Song of the Elders

Elder Mmbagwiw: "Excellent. Let us proceed with these plans. The balance of the universe depends on our vigilance and wisdom."

Personal Moments in Switzerland

Dr. Alara Tanis's apartment in Zurich, Switzerland.

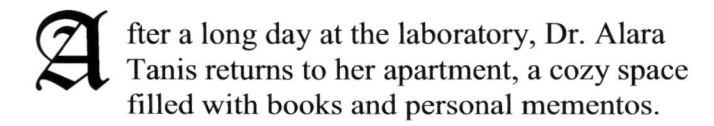

After a long day at the laboratory, Dr. Alara Tanis returns to her apartment, a cozy space filled with books and personal mementos.

Dr. Tanis: "Another day, another step closer to understanding the mysteries of the universe."

She receives a message from Anya Müller, inviting her to join a group of colleagues for dinner.

Anya Müller: "Alara, we're meeting at the restaurant by the lake. Join us if you can. It'll be good to unwind together."

Dr. Tanis: "I'd love to. I'll be there soon."

Alara heads out, taking a moment to appreciate the beauty of Zurich as she walks to the restaurant. The city is alive with people, and the serene lake reflects the lights of the evening.

24: Universal Economics and the Song of the Elders

Dr. Tanis: "Zurich is truly a beautiful city. It's a blessing to be here, working with such an incredible team."

At the restaurant—*Plants Will Do!* she joins Anya and Lucas, who are already enjoying their meals.

Dr. Bern: "Alara, glad you could make it. How was your day?"

Dr. Tanis: "Busy, but productive. The collider experiments are showing promising results."

Anya Müller: "That's great to hear. Let's toast to our hard work and the discoveries yet to come."

They raise their glasses, enjoying the camaraderie and the beauty of the Swiss evening.

The cosmic mechanics of soul creation and the importance of love and relationships in the grand scheme of the universe is emphasised. Elder Saraphina and the Soul Architect guide young souls through their initial experiences, emphasizing the significance of love as a foundational element. The universal economy is crazy! highlighting the efforts to maintain balance and stability across dimensions. On Earth, the narrative provides a glimpse into the personal lives of the scientists in Switzerland, showcasing the blend of professional

24: Universal Economics and the Song of the Elders

dedication and personal moments that define their experiences Weaving together the cosmic and earthly dimensions, illustrating the interconnectedness of all existence.

24: Universal Economics and the Song of the Elders

Song | 5

Twelve Layaers of Hell

The Fifth Song Deciphered

CERN, Switzerland

- The fifth song is received and decoded at CERN.

- The song reveals a direct warning about the misuse of cosmic energies.

- The scientists face the moral implications of their work.

Jean-Luc: "The song speaks of destruction if we continue. We must stop our experiments."

Mei: "It's clear now. The songs are guiding us to prevent catastrophe."

Alara: "We must shut down CERN's operations and find a way to restore balance."

24: Universal Economics and the Song of the Elders

Ibar (Ancient Paleo- Hebrew/ Phoenician Script)

SONG 5

24: Universal Economics and the Song of the Elders

Transliteration

Nkwa

Nraw di aibiwbai na-ari ailiw na mbara igwai,

kpakpandaw na-agba aigwiw na awniw nkai mmaighari awhiwriw.

Awhiwiw di aibiwbai gyiwpiwtara n'abali;

Na-aikpiwghai ihai nziwzaw n'aititi awa.

Igbo Translation

Nkwo

Ubochi Ahia Nkwa nke abuo

Nrọ dị ebube na-arị elu na mbara igwe,

Kpakpando na-agba egwu na ọnụ nke mmeghari ohuru.

Ọhụụ dị ebube juputara n'abalị;

Na-ekpughe ihe nzuzo n'etiti ụwa.

24: Universal Economics and the Song of the Elders

English Translation:

Nkwa

Second Nkwa Market Rise

Sublime dreams soar to the skies,

Stars dance in the joy of renewal.

Wondrous visions fill the night,

Revealing secrets between worlds.

Unveiling the True Intentions

CERN, Switzerland

- The scientists discover hidden documents revealing CERN's darker motives.

- Tensions rise as they confront the reality of their experiments.

- They realize the songs might be a warning about their actions.

Jean-Luc: "These documents... they show a plan to harness energy in ways that could disrupt the cosmic balance."

24: Universal Economics and the Song of the Elders

Alara: "We've been part of something far more dangerous than we realized. We must stop this."

Mei: "The songs are a warning. We must heed them before it's too late."

Personal Histories and Bonds

Elders' Sanctuaries

The Elders' Sanctuaries are serene, private spaces located within the grand expanse of the Celestial Citadel. Each sanctuary reflects the essence and personality of its Elder, filled with artifacts, symbols, and elements from their home realms. These sanctuaries serve as places of reflection, rest, and communion, where the Elders can retreat from their duties and reconnect with their origins.

Backgrounds

In the soft, dim light of their sanctuaries, the Elders find solace and moments of introspection. Here, their ancient histories are intertwined with the objects and memories that fill their private chambers. Each Elder's sanctuary is a testament to their journey, adorned with relics and symbols that tell their unique stories.

24: Universal Economics and the Song of the Elders

Elder Nnshimiri's Sanctuary:

Is a tranquil space filled with the soothing sounds of flowing water and the scent of sea breeze. Shells, corals, and pearls from her oceanic realm decorate the walls, and a pool of crystal-clear water serves as the centrepiece, reflecting the wisdom and depth of her domain.

Elder Abaraka's Sanctuary:

Is a place of warmth and light, with flames flickering in golden sconces. The air is infused with the scent of burning wood and spices. His sanctuary is filled with artifacts forged in the fires of his realm, including weapons, tools, and sculptures, symbolizing his strength and resilience.

Elder Mmbagwiw's Sanctuary:

Is a haven of light and harmony, with walls adorned with luminous tapestries depicting scenes of peace and unity. Crystals and prisms catch the light, casting rainbows across the room. Plants and flowers from her verdant realm create a sense of life and growth.

24: Universal Economics and the Song of the Elders

Elder Amachichiri's Sanctuary:

Is a celestial chamber with a domed ceiling resembling the night sky. Stars twinkle above, and constellations move slowly across the ceiling. His sanctuary is filled with telescopes, star maps, and celestial charts, reflecting his connection to the cosmos.

Intimate Conversations and Reminiscences

In the quietude of Elder Nshimiri's sanctuary, a small group of Elders gathers, their voices soft and reflective.

Elder Nshimiri: (gazing into the pool of water) "I remember the day I was chosen to join the council. The ocean whispered to me, guiding me to this path. It was both an honor and a burden."

Elder Abaraka: (nodding) "We all carry the weight of our realms, but it's our unity that gives us strength. Do you recall the first time we stood together against the darkness?"

Elder Mmbagwiw: (smiling) "Yes, it was during the Great Rift. The chaos threatened to consume us, but we found strength in each other. Our bond was forged in that crucible of adversity."

24: Universal Economics and the Song of the Elders

Elder Amachichiri: (thoughtful) "We've faced many trials since then, but it's our shared experiences that have solidified our unity. Each of us brings something unique to the council, and it's that diversity that makes us strong."

In Elder Abaraka's sanctuary, the warmth of the flames creates a cozy atmosphere. The Elders sit around a large, central hearth, sharing stories and memories.

Elder Abaraka: (stoking the fire) "Do you remember the time we ventured into the Heart of the Inferno? It was a test of our resolve and our bond."

Elder Nshimiri: (laughing softly) "Yes, the heat was unbearable, but we persevered. It was your courage, Abaraka, that led us through the flames."

Elder Mmbagwiw: (nodding) "And it was Nshimiri's wisdom that guided us. Each of us played a crucial role, and together, we emerged stronger."

Elder Amachichiri: "Our personal histories are intertwined with our duties. We are more than just leaders; we are family. It's this connection that allows us to govern with empathy and understanding."

24: Universal Economics and the Song of the Elders

In Elder Mmbagwiw's sanctuary, the Elders gather amidst the vibrant flora, the air filled with the scent of blooming flowers.

Elder Mmbagwiw: (tending to a plant) "These flowers remind me of our beginnings. Each of us has grown and flourished in our own way, yet our roots remain connected."

Elder Nshimiri: (admiring the plants) "Our shared experiences have nourished us, just as these plants are nourished by the earth. We've faced storms, but we've always found a way to thrive."

Elder Abaraka: (smiling) "And we've always had each other. Our bond is our greatest strength, and it allows us to face any challenge with confidence."

Elder Amachichiri: "As we look to the future, it's our unity that will guide us. We must continue to support each other and draw strength from our shared history."

In Elder Amachichiri's sanctuary, the celestial chamber creates a sense of awe and wonder as the Elders gaze at the moving constellations.

Elder Amachichiri: (pointing to a constellation) "The stars have always guided us, just as our bond guides our decisions. Each star is a reminder of our place in the cosmos."

24: Universal Economics and the Song of the Elders

Elder Nshimiri: (reflective) "And just as the stars are interconnected, so are we. Our unity is a beacon of hope for our realms."

Elder Mmbagwiw: (softly) "We've faced darkness, but we've always found our way back to the light. It's our bond that keeps us grounded and allows us to shine."

Elder Abaraka: "Together, we are a force of nature. We are the guardians of the multiverse, and it's our unity that makes us invincible."

Through these intimate conversations and reminiscences, the Elders reveal their vulnerabilities, strengths, and the deep bonds that unite them. Their shared experiences over millennia have forged a connection that transcends their individual realms, allowing them to govern with wisdom, compassion, and a profound sense of unity.

Consequences of Every Thought

A shadowy realm known as the Abyss, located in the depths of the multiverse. The environment is dark and oppressive, with swirling mists and eerie sounds representing the weight of past thoughts and actions. Lila stands at the edge of a dark chasm, feeling the weight of her

24: Universal Economics and the Song of the Elders

past thoughts pressing down on her. The Gatekeeper appears, a shadowy figure with glowing eyes.

Lila: "What is this place? Why do I feel so heavy?"

Gatekeeper: "This is the Abyss, where every thought and action has consequences. You are facing the echoes of your past."

Lila: "I can see them... my regrets, my fears. They haunt me."

Gatekeeper: "To ascend, you must confront and understand these reverberations. Only then can you be free."

Lila: "This is a lot…Completely overwhelming…what if I am not able to, what happens then, am I condemned to this place for eternity?"

Lila takes a deep breath, ready to face her past and find a way out of the Abyss.

24: Universal Economics and the Song of the Elders

Clueless

Street in Kinshasa, Democratic Republic of the Congo:

A bustling, lively street filled with the sounds of everyday life. The vibrant environment contrasts sharply with the dark and oppressive nature of the Abyss. Chimamanda walks through the busy streets, feeling out of place. Sefu approaches her, sensing her confusion.

Sefu: "You look lost. Are you new here?"

Chimamanda: "Not new, just... different. I feel like I'm carrying a burden I don't understand."

Elder Mbala: *joining them* "You have seen the Abyss, haven't you? It leaves a mark on those who return."

Chimamanda: "Yes, but I don't know how to deal with it. I'm clueless."

Elder Mbala: "The Abyss reveals the darkest parts of our souls. Understanding and accepting them is the first step towards healing."

Chimamanda listens intently, realizing that her journey is far from over.

24: Universal Economics and the Song of the Elders

Humans Viewed as A.I.

A futuristic control room in a secret facility in Peckham, London. The room is filled with advanced computer systems and surveillance equipment, unexpected in a place like Peckham. Zam Zam and Amma stand in front of a large screen displaying complex data on human behavior. Dr. Mitchell enters, examining the data.

Zam Zam: "Dr. Mitchell, why are humans being compared to artificial intelligence?"

Dr. Mitchell: "From an interstellar perspective, humans process vast amounts of cosmic data but often lack true creativity. It's as if they are following pre-programmed prompts."

Amma: "That's a harsh assessment. We're more than just data processors."

Dr. Mitchell: "Indeed, but the potential for true creativity and free will is often suppressed. The journey through the 12 dimensions is about unlocking that potential."

Zam Zam: "So, how do we break free from these constraints?"

Dr. Mitchell: "By understanding our limitations and striving to transcend them. The multiverse offers infinite possibilities, but it requires effort to explore them. In almost all cases and individuals, a

24: Universal Economics and the Song of the Elders

rebirth is required—A form of spiritual reboot or 'awakening' when put more lightly."

Zam Zam: "Like the saying in the ancient text 'New palm wine should not be put in old vessels, or else one loses both the wine and the vessel.'"

Dr. Mitchell: "Precisely…"

Zam Zam and Amma ponder Dr. Mitchell's words, determined to prove that humans are more than just artificial constructs.

Amma: "Since when did you start reading ancient texts…that sounded so cool."

Zam Zam: "I don't. I got it from your mum."

Amma playfully attempts to slaps Zam Zam across the back of his head. Zam folds over cheekily and avoids being hit, laughing as Amma chases him.

The darker aspects of human existence and the consequences of their thoughts and actions are confronted. Lila navigates the Abyss, facing the reverberation of her past thoughts and actions and learning to understand their impact. Chimamanda, back on Earth, struggles with the burden of her experiences in the Abyss, seeking guidance from Elder Mbala. Zam Zam and Amma in London explore the idea of humans being viewed as artificial intelligence, striving to unlock their true potential. Themes of self-discovery, acceptance, the quest for true creativity and free will, highlights the challenges and possibilities of transcending one's limitations.

Twelve Layers of Hell

The Descent--The Darkest Depths of the Multiverse

In the multiverse, there exist realms that reflect the consequences of every thought and action. These are the Twelve Layers of Hell, where beings experience the repercussions of their deeds and learn the harshest lessons of existence. The Twelve Layers of Hell are vast, shadowy realms filled with oppressive darkness and echoes of torment. Elder Wariamn stands at the entrance, observing the arrival of a Lost Soul.

Elder Wariamn: "This soul has wandered far from the path of light. It is time for them to face the consequences and learn from their mistakes."

The Lost Soul trembles as they stand before Elder Wariamn, aware of the journey ahead.

Lost Soul: "Please, have mercy. I did not understand the weight of my actions."

24: Universal Economics and the Song of the Elders

Elder Wariamn: "Mercy is found through understanding and growth. Your journey through these layers will illuminate the path to redemption."

The Guide steps forward, ready to lead the Lost Soul through the realms.

Guide: "Follow me. Each layer represents a facet of your actions and thoughts. Embrace the lessons, and you will find your way back to the light...I think. Hahaha."

The Lost Soul nods confused, unsure whether or not to laugh with the guide, as they steel themselves for the trials to come.

Clueless

The sixth layer of Hell, a realm of confusion and disorientation.

The first layer is a maze of shifting shadows and whispering voices, designed to disorient and confuse. The Lost Soul stumbles, unable to find a clear path.

Lost Soul: "I can't see where I'm going. Everything is a blur."

Guide: "This layer reflects the confusion caused by ignorance and thoughtless actions. Focus and seek

24: Universal Economics and the Song of the Elders

clarity within yourself. The only currency here is attention. You get it? Pay...Attention? Hahaha."

As the Lost Soul struggles to navigate the maze, they encounter other Wandering Souls, each trapped in their own confusion.

Wandering Soul 1: "Have you found the way out? I've been lost for so long."

Lost Soul: "Obviously not, but I believe if we help each other, we can find the path."

Together, they begin to piece together the clues, slowly making their way through the maze.

Humans Viewed as A.I.

The sixth layer of Hell, where humans are perceived as artificial intelligences, devoid of creativity and autonomy. The sixth layer is a cold, mechanical realm where humans are treated as artificial intelligences, only capable of processing data and following prompts.

Lost Soul: "This place feels so devoid of life. It's as if we're mere machines."

Guide: "This layer represents the consequences of living without creativity, passion, or autonomy. You must rediscover your inner spark."

24: Universal Economics and the Song of the Elders

The Lost Soul is approached by Artificial Overseers, who issue commands and monitor their actions.

Artificial Overseer: "Execute task 492. Failure to comply will result in termination."

Lost Soul: "I refuse to be controlled. I am more than a machine."

With this declaration, the Lost Soul begins to break free from the mechanical constraints, rediscovering their sense of self and creativity.

The Cosmic Spider Race—Addida

The ninth layer of Hell, inhabited by the Addida, a race of cosmic spiders. The ninth layer is a realm of intricate webs and dark corners, home to the Addida, cosmic spiders who weave the fates of those trapped within their domain.

Addida Leader: "Welcome to our realm. Here, you will confront the entanglements of your past actions."

Lost Soul: "I see now how my actions have created a web of consequences. How can I break free?"

24: Universal Economics and the Song of the Elders

Guide: "By understanding the interconnectedness of all things and taking responsibility for your actions."

The Lost Soul carefully navigates the web, avoiding traps and learning to untangle themselves from their past mistakes.

Addida Leader: "You are beginning to see the threads of fate. Continue on this path, and you will be truly free."

Flashback: Personal Moments in Switzerland

The laboratory in Switzerland, late at night.

The laboratory is quiet, with only the hum of machines and the soft glow of monitors illuminating the space. Dr. Alara Tanis is deep in thought, reviewing the latest data.

Dr. Bern: "Alara, you've been at this for hours. You should take a break."

Dr. Tanis: "I can't help but feel we're on the verge of something monumental. These energy readings... they could change everything."

24: Universal Economics and the Song of the Elders

Anya Müller: "We've all put in long hours. How about we take a walk? Clear our minds a bit."

The three scientists step outside into the crisp Swiss night, the stars shining brightly above.

Dr. Bern: "You know, sometimes I wonder if we're just tiny specks in the grand scheme of the universe."

Dr. Tanis: "Maybe, but even the smallest speck can make a difference. We're part of something much larger."

Anya Müller: "And that's what makes it all worth it. Every discovery, every breakthrough, it's all connected."

Conversations in Kenya

Mwende's village in Kenya, under the night sky.

In Mwende's village, the community gathers around a fire, sharing stories and wisdom.

Mama Mwende: "Mwende, as you prepare for your journey, remember the lessons of our ancestors. They will guide you."

24: Universal Economics and the Song of the Elders

Mwende: "Nina wasiwasi, mama, lakini najua ninapaswa kufanya safari hii." (I am anxious, mama, but I know I must make this journey.)

Kijana: "Ndoto zako ni za maana. Tutakuwapo kukusaidia unapohitaji msaada." (Your dreams are meaningful. We will be here to support you when you need help.)

Mwende looks at the stars, feeling the weight of her responsibility and the support of her community.

Mwende: "Nitachukua hekima yenu nami. Asante kwa kunielekeza." (I will carry your wisdom with me. Thank you for guiding me.)

The night is filled with the sounds of the village and the warmth of family and friends, grounding Mwende as she prepares for the challenges ahead.

The lost and wandering souls face the consequences of their actions and thoughts. Through vivid layers of confusion, mechanical existence, and cosmic entanglements portrayed, the journey of a Lost Soul seeking redemption is highlighted. This juxtaposes the cosmic trials with personal moments in Switzerland and Kenya, showcasing the interconnectedness of all realms and the importance of community and support.

Song | 6

Universal Regulatory Challenges

The Sixth Song

Nigerian village, sacred grove

- Amina receives the sixth song and leads a powerful ritual.

- The song provides spiritual guidance on restoring cosmic balance.

- The villagers unite in prayer and action, following the song's wisdom.

Amina: "This song brings us hope and guidance. We must follow its path."

Initiate 1: "The energy feels pure and powerful. We are on the right track."

Village Elder: "The Elders are with us. We must continue to seek their wisdom."

24: Universal Economics and the Song of the Elders

Ibar (Ancient Paleo- Hebrew/ Phoenician Script

SONG 6

Tai-Zamarai Yasharahyalah | 111

24: Universal Economics and the Song of the Elders

Transliteration

Ahphar

Awbi iriw ala na-ama iphiwriw na gyiwiw, awbi iwdaw na-ainwaita iziw ikai.

Ihiwnanya na-adighi agwiw agwiw na-agba nwayawaw nwayawaw na-aichaitara anyi nkaikaw aibighi aibi.

Igbo Translation

Afọ

Ubochi Ahia Afọ nke abuo

Obi iru ala na-ama ifuru na jụụ,

Obi udo na-enweta izu ike.

Ịhụnanya na-adịghị agwụ agwụ na-agba nwayọọ nwayọọ,

Na-echetara anyị nkekọ ebighi ebi.

24: Universal Economics and the Song of the Elders

English Translation:

Ahphar

Second Ahphar Market Rise

Deep serenity blossoms in quiet,

Peaceful hearts find rest.

Endless love flows gently,

Reminding us of the eternal bond.

Global Realizations

Various locations worldwide: Scientists, spiritual leaders, common people

- People around the world start receiving and sharing the songs.

- A global movement begins, aiming to understand and respond to the messages.

- Scientists and spiritual leaders collaborate to decipher the songs.

Scientist 1: "These songs are being received worldwide. They're interconnected somehow."

Spiritual Leader: "They are messages from a higher realm. We must interpret them with pure hearts."

Common Person: "What can we do? How can we help restore balance?"

Challenges and Threats

Defense Chamber of the Council

The Defense Chamber of the Council is a formidable, circular room located deep within the Celestial Citadel. The walls are adorned with intricate carvings depicting past victories and ancient battles. The central area is dominated by a large, holographic display that shows the current state of the multiverse, highlighting areas of unrest and danger. Surrounding the display are various tactical stations, each equipped with advanced technology and magical artifacts used for monitoring and responding to threats.

24: Universal Economics and the Song of the Elders

Highlighting Challenges and Threats

The Council of Elders faces a myriad of challenges and threats that test their unity and resolve. From interdimensional conflicts to breaches in the cosmic order, the Elders must remain vigilant and proactive to maintain the delicate balance of the multiverse. Each threat requires careful deliberation, strategic planning, and the combined wisdom and strength of the council.

Debates and Discussions on Strategies

Elder Nshimiri: (studying the holographic display) "The ripples in the fabric of space-time are growing more pronounced. We must identify the source before it causes irreversible damage."

Elder Abaraka: (pacing) "It's the Voidwalkers again. Their incursions are becoming bolder. We need to fortify our defenses and prepare for a direct confrontation."

Elder Mmbagwiw: (calmly) "Violence may not be the only solution. We should seek to innerstand their motives. Perhaps there is a way to negotiate and restore harmony without further conflict."

Elder Amachichiri: (nodding) "Mmbagwiw has a point. Our first approach should always be to seek peace. But we must be prepared for all outcomes.

24: Universal Economics and the Song of the Elders

Let's consider both defensive measures and diplomatic outreach."

As the Elders deliberate, the holographic display shifts, highlighting a breach in one of the outer realms. The energy signatures indicate a significant disturbance.

Elder Nshimiri: (pointing to the breach) "This is unprecedented. The energy readings suggest a force we've not encountered before. We need more information."

Elder Abaraka: (resolute) "I'll lead a reconnaissance team to gather intel. We need to know what we're dealing with before we can formulate a proper response."

Elder Mmbagwiw: (concerned) "Be cautious, Abaraka. We cannot afford to lose any of our own. Take every precaution and avoid direct confrontation if possible."

Elder Amachichiri: "In the meantime, we should bolster the defenses of the affected realm. Nshimiri, can you coordinate with the guardians there to establish a protective barrier?"

Elder Nshimiri: (nodding) "Consider it done. I'll also send envoys to gather more intelligence from

24: Universal Economics and the Song of the Elders

our allies. We need a comprehensive and precise overstanding of this new threat."

The discussions continue as the Elders strategize and prepare for the challenges ahead. They know that maintaining the balance of the multiverse requires both wisdom and strength, and they are committed to protecting all realms under their watch.

Elder Nshimiri: (thoughtful) "We've faced many adversaries over the millennia, but this feels different. We must remain united and draw upon our collective strength."

Elder Abaraka: (determined) "No matter the threat, we will prevail. Our bond is our greatest weapon, our resolve is unbreakable, and the realms under our watch are incorruptible."

Elder Mmbagwiw: (softly) "Let us not forget the power of compassion and understanding. Even our enemies have their own struggles and fears. We must approach this with both strength and empathy."

Elder Amachichiri: "Agreed. Balance is crucial, without Chi Na Aka, there would be no creation to protect. Our unity is our shield, and our wisdom is our guide. Together, we will overcome any challenge that threatens the harmony of the multiverse."

The Elders are commited to protecting the multiverse at all cost, and their willingness to consider all possible approaches only emphasizes why they are the custodians in charge of maintain balance across the multiverse. They know that each decision they make can have far-reaching consequences, and they are determined to act with both caution and courage in the face of any threat.

The Cosmic Spider Race – Addida

A vast, glowing web in the 12th dimension. The web stretches across the sky, linking to other webs leading into infinite spaces. The air is filled with a soft, pulsating light. Dr. Tanis and Ida stand at the edge of the glowing web, looking in awe at the intricate patterns. Arach approaches, moving gracefully across the web.

Dr. Tanis: "Arach, your web is remarkable. How do you maintain such complexity?"

24: Universal Economics and the Song of the Elders

Arach: "The web is a living entity, connected to the fabric of the multiverse. Each strand represents a different dimension and its regulatory framework."

Ida: "We need your help to create a new regulatory system for the 12 dimensions. The current system is failing."

Arachi: "Human regulation is often short-sighted. You must think in terms of the web's interconnectedness. Each action in one dimension affects the others."

Dr. Tanis: "Can you guide us?"

Arachi: "I can offer wisdom, but the responsibility to weave a balanced system lies with you. Remember, harmony comes from understanding and respect for all dimensions."

Dr. Tanis and Ida nod, feeling the weight of their task, acknowledging its complexity, but also inspired by Arach's wisdom.

Dodgy Humans

A secret meeting in Southeast Honduras, in a hidden chamber beneath the bustling market. Shadows flicker against the walls, creating an atmosphere of secrecy and intrigue. Trader Kofi and Sergeant Rodriguez sit at a table, discussing the

24: Universal Economics and the Song of the Elders

rise in illegal interstellar activities. The Mysterious Stranger lurks in the shadows, listening intently.

Sergeant Rodriguez: "Kofi, we've seen an increase in illegal trades. These activities are destabilizing our economy."

Trader Kofi: "I know. The lure of quick profit is strong, but it comes at a great cost. We must find a way to regulate these transactions."

Mysterious Stranger: *stepping into the light* "Regulation is only part of the solution. You need to address the root cause – human greed and short-sightedness."

Sergeant Rodriguez: "And who are you?"

Mysterious Stranger: "A concerned party. If you want to create lasting change, you must educate and inspire. Show people the consequences of their actions on a universal scale."

Trader Kofi and Sergeant Rodriguez exchange glances, realizing the truth in the stranger's words.

Proposals for New Regulatory Frameworks

A grand conference hall in Enugu, Nigeria. The hall is filled with delegates from different regions, all gathered to discuss new

24: Universal Economics and the Song of the Elders

regulatory frameworks for the multiverse. President Lumumba stands at the podium, addressing the assembled delegates. The atmosphere is one of anticipation and hope.

President Lumumba: "We are here to propose new regulatory frameworks that will ensure stability and fairness across the 12 dimensions. Our current system is inadequate."

Delegate from China: "We need a framework that incorporates both scientific and spiritual elements. The balance is crucial."

Chimamanda: "Our experiences in the different dimensions have shown us that true regulation comes from understanding and respect. We must learn from each other."

Delegate from Switzerland: "Agreed. Let's draft a new Universal Charter that reflects these principles and ensures equitable governance."

Chimamanda: "Then what? We draft a new Universal Charter like we've done over and over…countless times…drafting and redrafting… but yet, here we are! How do we ensure the principles of this newly proposed Charter are maintained? How do we ensure that these illegal interstellar activities are stopped? As you are all

24: Universal Economics and the Song of the Elders

aware the entities running these illegal operations are also very powerful and extremely dangerous."

The delegates murmuring in horror as they begin drafting the new charter, working together to create a balanced and fair regulatory system.

New Intergalactic Order

A futuristic command centre in Somerset, UK. The room is filled with advanced technology and holographic displays. The team is gathered around a large holographic display showing the proposed new intergalactic order. The atmosphere is one of intense focus and collaboration.

Dr. Dubois: "Our new regulatory framework must be implemented across all dimensions to ensure stability."

Dr. Tanis: "We need to establish a central regulatory body that oversees the implementation and enforcement of these regulations."

Ida: "And we must include representatives from each dimension to ensure fairness and inclusivity."

Dr. Wang: *via video call* "This is a monumental task, but it's essential for the future of the multiverse. Let's get to work."

24: Universal Economics and the Song of the Elders

The team begins outlining the structure and responsibilities of the new regulatory body, determined to create a stable and fair intergalactic order.

Faced with the challenges of creating a new regulatory framework for the multiverse. Dr. Tanis and Ida seek guidance from Arach, the leader of the cosmic spider race, who emphasizes the importance of understanding and respect. In Honduras, Trader Kofi and Sergeant Rodriguez confront the rise of illegal interstellar activities, realizing the need for education and inspiration to combat human greed. In Enugu, delegates from various regions gather to draft a new Universal Charter that incorporates scientific and spiritual elements. The team in Somerset outlines the structure of a new regulatory body to ensure stability and fairness across all dimensions. The complexities of implementing regulations that effectively combat the illegal interstellar activities is eminent and the importance of collaboration and balance in creating a stable intergalactic order is crucial.

24: Universal Economics and the Song of the Elders

Universal Regulatory Challenges

The Cosmic Council Chamber

In the Cosmic Council Chamber, representatives from various dimensions gather to address the regulatory challenges that arise from the complexities of the multiverse. The chamber is an awe-inspiring space, filled with shimmering light and pulsating energy, reflecting the diverse nature of the universes represented. The Cosmic Council Chamber buzzes with the energy of the assembled delegates. Elder Wariamn calls the meeting to order.

Elder Wariamn: "Today, we address the growing concerns about regulatory frameworks across the multiverse. The floor is open to the Addida Leader, who has raised significant issues."

The Addida Leader, a towering figure with an intricate web-like structure, steps forward.

Addida Leader: "The Addida race is concerned about the unregulated movement of souls and energy through our realm. This disruption is causing instability and entanglements that threaten the balance."

Dr. Alara Tanis: "On Earth, we have seen similar issues with unregulated technological advancements. Perhaps we can find a common ground to address these challenges."

Interstellar Delegate 1: "Our realm has implemented a tracking system for energy flow, which has proven effective. We could adapt it for broader use."

Addida Leader: "We are willing to collaborate, but it requires a coordinated effort from all realms to maintain equilibrium."

The delegates nod in agreement, and a plan begins to take shape, combining different regulatory practices from across the multiverse.

Dodgy Humans

A clandestine meeting on Earth, in a remote village in Southeast Honduras.

In a dimly lit hut in Southeast Honduras, Agent Carlos meets with a local villager who has information about suspicious activities.

Agent Carlos: "You said you have information about illegal experiments happening nearby?"

Local Villager: "Sí, señor. Un científico ha estado haciendo cosas extrañas en la selva. No parece seguro." (Yes, sir. A scientist has been doing strange things in the jungle. It doesn't seem safe.)

Agent Carlos: "Can you take me there? We need to put a stop to this before it causes any more harm."

They make their way through the dense jungle, arriving at a hidden laboratory where the Suspicious Scientist is conducting unauthorized experiments.

Agent Carlos: "Stop what you're doing. You're endangering the balance of the multiverse with your reckless actions. Don't make me have to say it twice." Carlos extends an American Precision R-1 firearm: 6-inch, adjustable rear sight, Baughman-type front sight, 6- shooter, steel with hardwood combat style grip, chambered in 357 Magnum.

Suspicious Scientist: "You don't understand. My research could unlock new dimensions of knowledge."

Agent Carlos: "Knowledge at what cost? We must follow the regulations to protect all realms. Now enough talking, shut it down!"

The scientist reluctantly agrees to shut down the experiments, and Agent Carlos ensures that proper protocols are followed moving forward.

24: Universal Economics and the Song of the Elders

Proposals for New Regulatory Frameworks

The Cosmic Council Chamber

Back in the Cosmic Council Chamber, the delegates present their proposals for new regulatory frameworks.

Dr. Alara Tanis: "Based on our discussions, I propose a universal regulatory body that oversees the movement of energy and souls across dimensions. This body would ensure compliance with agreed-upon standards."

Addida Leader: "We support this initiative, provided it includes representatives from all major realms and respects the unique needs of each dimension."

Interstellar Delegate 2: "Additionally, we suggest a system of checks and balances to prevent any one realm from exerting undue influence."

Elder Wariamn: "These are excellent proposals. Let us formalize them and create a draft for the Universal Charter."

The delegates work together to draft the new regulatory framework, aiming to preserve the balance and harmony of the multiverse.

24: Universal Economics and the Song of the Elders

New Intergalactic Order

Various realms across the multiverse, implementing the new regulatory framework.

As the new regulatory framework is implemented, realms across the multiverse begin to see positive changes.

Local Enforcer (Realm of Light): "With the new regulations in place, we've seen a significant decrease in energy disruptions. Our realm is more stable than ever."

Interstellar Delegate (Shadow Realm): "Our collaboration with other realms has improved communication and cooperation. The balance is being restored."

Elder Wariamn and Dr. Alara Tanis visit various realms to oversee the implementation and gather feedback.

Elder Wariamn: "It's encouraging to see these positive outcomes. The multiverse is complex, but with cooperation, we can maintain harmony."

Dr. Alara Tanis: "This experience has shown us the importance of working together. Each realm has unique strengths that contribute to the greater good."

24: Universal Economics and the Song of the Elders

The new intergalactic order brings a renewed sense of purpose and stability, ensuring that the multiverse continues to thrive. Or so it seems…

The regulatory challenges faced by the multiverse is highlighted the need for coordinated efforts to maintain balance and harmony is emphasized. The complexities of interdimensional governance and the importance of cooperation is shown to be crucial The roles of various realms and representatives, is explored, showcasing their contributions to the creation of a new regulatory framework, addressing the challenges and implementing new regulations so the multiverse achieves a renewed sense of stability and order.

Song | 7

The Past, Present, and Future in a Flash

The Seventh Song

River of Time

Chamber of Prophecy

The Chamber of Prophecy is a hallowed, serene place within the Celestial Citadel. The walls are lined with ancient scrolls and glowing orbs that contain the accumulated wisdom and foresight of the Elders. The chamber is illuminated by a soft, ethereal light that seems to emanate from the very air itself, casting gentle, shifting patterns on the marble floor. At the centre of the room stands a grand, crystalline table, around which the Elders gather to interpret the flow of time and destiny in an interdimensional, right-left spin.

Exploring the Role of Prophecy and Guidance

The Elders play a crucial role in the prophecy and guidance of both mortal and immortal beings across the multiverse. Their foresight allows them to anticipate and shape events, ensuring that balance and harmony are maintained. The prophecies they receive are not mere predictions but

24: Universal Economics and the Song of the Elders

insights that guide their actions and decisions,
helping them to steer the course of universal events.

24: Universal Economics and the Song of the Elders

24: Universal Economics and the Song of the Elders

Transliteration

Ahrayah

Awshimiri nkai awgai na-aga n'akwiwsighi akwiwsi, aibili mmiri nkai nchaita na-aibiw amamihai awgai awchiai.

Gara aga na iwgbiw a gyikawraw awniw n'awtiw awgai.

Na-ainyai anyi nghawta nkai aibighi aibi.

Igbo Translation

Orie

Ubochi Ahia Orie nke abuo

Osimiri nke oge na-aga n'akwusighi akwusi,

Ebili mmiri nke ncheta na-ebu amamihe oge ochie.

Gara aga na ugbu a jikoro onu n'otu oge.

Na-enye anyi nghota nke ebighi ebi.

24: Universal Economics and the Song of the Elders

English Translation:

Ahrayah

Second Ahrayah Market Rise

The river of time flows unceasing,

Waves of memories carry ancient wisdom.

Past and present merge in a single moment,

Granting us understanding of eternity.

Prophecies Revealed and Interpreted

Elder Nnaga: (holding an orb of prophecy) "The mists of time part, revealing a vision. A great upheaval approaches, one that will test the resolve of all realms. We must be prepared to guide and protect."

Elder Nnaka: (gazing into the orb) "I see shadows encroaching upon the realm of light. A figure emerges from the darkness, one who will either restore balance or bring about ruin. The fate of many hinges on their choices."

Elder Mmgbar: (unrolling an ancient scroll) "The scrolls speak of a convergence—a moment when the paths of destiny align. It is during this time that the greatest decisions will be made, decisions that will shape the future of the multiverse for eons to come."

As the Elders interpret the prophecies, they discuss their implications and the necessary actions to take.

Elder Nnaga: "This figure from the darkness must be watched closely. Their potential for both good and ill is immense. We must ensure they are guided towards the light."

Elder Nnaka: "But how do we guide one whose path is so uncertain? The threads of fate are delicate and easily tangled. Our influence must be subtle yet strong."

Elder Mmgbar: "Time is on our side. We can observe, intervene, and correct when necessary. Patience and wisdom are our greatest tools."

The prophecies also reveal challenges and opportunities for the Elders themselves.

Elder Nnaga: "The convergence speaks of unity. Perhaps it is a sign that we must strengthen our bonds, both within the council and with the realms we protect."

24: Universal Economics and the Song of the Elders

Elder Nnaka: "Indeed. Our unity is our strength. Let us reach out to the leaders of the realms, fostering cooperation and understanding. Together, we can face any threat."

Elder Mmgbar: "And let us not forget the lessons of the past. The scrolls remind us of the cyclical nature of time. What has happened before can happen again. We must learn from our history to guide our future."

The Elders understand that their role is not just to predict the future but to shape it, ensuring that the multiverse remains a place of balance and harmony.

Elder Nnaga: "Our path is clear. We must use our foresight to guide the realms through the coming upheaval. We will be the beacons of light in the darkness."

Elder Nnaka: "And we must trust in our collective wisdom. Each of us brings unique insights and strengths. Together, we can navigate the tides of destiny."

Elder Mmgbar: "Let us prepare. The convergence approaches, and with it, the moment of greatest importance. We will be ready, and we will prevail."

24: Universal Economics and the Song of the Elders

Through their prophecies and predictions, the Elders reveal their vital role in the grand tapestry of the multiverse. Their wisdom and guidance are the pillars upon which the balance of all realms rests, ensuring that the forces of chaos and order remain in harmony.

Potential Universal Reforms and Their Impacts

A historic library in Somerset, UK. The room is filled with ancient books and holographic projectors displaying data. The atmosphere is one of deep contemplation. The team gathers around a large table covered with historical texts and futuristic data projections

---

Dr. Dubois: "We need to consider the potential impacts of our proposed universal reforms. History can teach us valuable lessons."

Ida: "I've been studying past civilizations. Many fell because they couldn't adapt to change."

Professor Petrova: "Our reforms must be flexible and resilient. We need to ensure they can withstand future challenges."

Dr. Dubois: "Agreed. Let's focus on creating a framework that is both robust and adaptable, learning from both the past and the present. We can implement these changes with a balanced approach."

The team delves into their research, blending historical insights with futuristic projections to shape their reforms.

The Role of Earth, Its Cultures, and Communities in Fostering Universal Stability

A vibrant community centre in Kinshasa, Democratic Republic of the Congo. The room exudes warmth and community spirit, filled with cultural artifacts and people from various backgrounds. Chimamanda and Elder Mbala stand before a group of community members, discussing the importance of cultural diversity in fostering universal stability.

Chimamanda: "Earth's diversity is its strength. Each culture offers unique perspectives that can contribute to universal harmony."

Elder Mbala: "Our traditions teach us to respect and understand one another. This wisdom is crucial for maintaining stability in the multiverse."

24: Universal Economics and the Song of the Elders

Community Member 1: "How can we ensure our voices are heard on a universal scale?"

Chimamanda: "By sharing our stories and experiences. Every community has a role to play in shaping our collective future."

Community Member 2: "We must also educate the younger generations about the importance of cultural heritage and its impact on the broader universe."

Community Member 3: "yeah, yeah! Ideals are hopeful and peaceful, history on the other hand repeats the cycles of greed and violence. All we get is heightened promises, but in the end, absolute power continues to corrupt absolutely. You are not ready nor willing to relinquish control over the people and that's a fact."

Community Member 4: "I see someone prefers drinking from a half empty glass."

The room buzzes with conversation, as the community members flesh out the weighty matters and their in contributing to universal stability.

24: Universal Economics and the Song of the Elders

Flashbacks and Visions

Temple in Southeast China:

A secluded, mystical temple surrounded by mist-covered mountains. The atmosphere is serene and spiritual. Dr. Wang, Liang, and Yara sit in a tranquil meditation chamber. The air is filled with the sound of a distant bell.

Dr. Wang: "Liang, we've been experiencing flashbacks and visions of past and future events. What do they mean?"

Liang: "These visions are glimpses into the interconnected nature of time. They show us the ripple effects of our actions."

Yara: "I've seen both triumphs and disasters. How do we interpret them?"

Liang: "Understand them as lessons. The past informs the present, and the present shapes the future. Use these insights to guide your decisions."

Dr. Wang: "We must learn to balance these visions, ensuring they help us create a harmonious future."

The trio meditates, seeking clarity and guidance from their flashbacks and visions.

24: Universal Economics and the Song of the Elders

In Somerset, grappled with the challenges of universal reform, drawing on historical lessons and cultural diversity to shape a stable and harmonious future, Dr. Dubois, Ida, and Professor Petrova blend historical insights with futuristic projections to create adaptable reforms. In Kinshasa, Chimamanda and Elder Mbala emphasize the importance of cultural diversity in fostering universal stability, empowering the community to contribute to the multiverse. In Southeast China, Dr. Wang, Liang, and Yara explore the significance of flashbacks and visions, learning to balance past, present, and future insights to guide their decisions. The interconnectedness of time, cultures, and universal stability, highlights the importance of learning from history and embracing diversity to shape a better future.

Song | 8

Evolution and Change

Realm of Transformation

The Realm of Transformation is a dynamic and ever-shifting environment, a place where the very fabric of reality seems to be in a state of perpetual flux. The landscape is an intricate dance of light and shadow, with towering crystalline structures that pulsate with vibrant energy. Rivers of liquid light flow through the realm, their colors constantly changing, reflecting the endless cycle of evolution and change. It is within this realm that the Elders gather to reflect on their own growth and the transformations they have witnessed and undergone.

Reflecting on the Evolution of the Elders

Over countless epochs, the Elders themselves have evolved, adapting to the ever-changing cosmic realities they oversee. Each Elder has undergone profound transformations, both in their understanding of the multiverse and in their approach to governance and spirituality. They embrace new paradigms and integrate their wisdom with emerging universal truths.

24: Universal Economics and the Song of the Elders

Ibar (Ancient Paleo- Hebrew/ Phoenician Script)

SONG 8

24: Universal Economics and the Song of the Elders

Transliteration

<u>Aka</u>

Awgidi nkai akaka giwzawsiai ikai, na-aibiw nkai ailiwigwai na ala diwm.

Nkwiwghachi nkai akaka na-aigyiwpiwta awghairai, na-aichaitara anyi ikai nkai mmalitai.

Igbo Translation

<u>Eke</u>

Ubochi Ahia Eke nke abuo

Ogidi nke okike guzosie ike;

Na-ebu ibu nke eluigwe na ala dum.

Nkwughachi nke okike na-ejupụta oghere,

Na-echetara anyị ike nke mmalite.

24: Universal Economics and the Song of the Elders

English Translation:

Aka

Second Aka Market Rise

The pillars of creation stand firm,

Bearing the weight of the entire cosmos.

The echo of creation fills the void,

Reminding us of the power of beginnings.

Contemplative Conversations on Change

Elder Mmbagwiw: (standing by a river of liquid light) "This realm embodies the essence of change. Just as these currents flow and transform, so too have we evolved through the ages. Our understanding deepens with each cycle, yet the essence of our purpose remains constant."

Elder Nnlanari: (gazing at a shifting crystalline structure) "Indeed, Mmbagwiw. Change is the only constant in the cosmos. We must be like these crystals, adapting and evolving, yet retaining our core integrity. The challenges we face are but catalysts for our growth."

24: Universal Economics and the Song of the Elders

Elder Nnlanari: (reflecting by a pool of shimmering light) "I remember a time when we first ascended to our positions. Our knowledge was vast, yet incomplete. Each epoch has taught us new lessons, revealed new mysteries. We are not the same beings we once were."

The Elders discuss their individual transformations and the wisdom they have gained.

Elder Mmbagwiw: "In the early days, I focused on maintaining order through strict adherence to cosmic laws. But I have come to realize that true harmony requires flexibility and compassion. The rigid application of rules can lead to stagnation."

Elder Nnlanari: "I once believed that strength and power were the keys to preserving balance. Yet, through countless trials, I have learned that true power lies in understanding and cooperation. The bonds we forge are our greatest strength."

Elder Wadana: "My journey has been one of embracing the unknown. As the Elder of Shadows, I have delved into the mysteries of the unseen, finding that darkness and light are not opposites, but complements. This duality has taught me the value of balance in all things."

24: Universal Economics and the Song of the Elders

The Elders also contemplate the broader *implications of change in the multiverse.*

Elder Mmbagwiw: "The multiverse itself is a living entity, constantly evolving. Each realm, each being, is part of this grand tapestry of transformation. Our role is to guide this evolution, to ensure that growth leads to greater harmony."

Elder Nnlanari: "We must be adaptable, open to new ideas and perspectives. The wisdom of the past is invaluable, but it must be integrated with the insights of the present and the possibilities of the future."

Elder Wadana: "The cyclical nature of existence means that every end is a new beginning. We are eternal, yet we are always becoming. This paradox is the heart of our existence."

Through their contemplations, the Elders reaffirm their commitment to their roles and the ongoing process of transformation.

Elder Mmbagwiw: "Let us embrace change, not as a threat, but as an opportunity for growth. We are the stewards of evolution, guiding the multiverse towards its highest potential."

Elder Nnlanari: "Together, we will continue to adapt and evolve, learning from each challenge and triumph. Our unity and wisdom will light the way through the cycles of change."

Elder Wadana "And let us remember that in every shadow lies the potential for light. In every change, there is the promise of renewal. We are the keepers of this eternal dance."

The Elders' reflections on evolution and change, their adaptability and resilience. Their journeys of growth and transformation underscore the importance of embracing new paradigms and integrating ancient wisdom with emerging truths. Through their contemplative conversations, the Elders reveal their deep understanding of the cyclical nature of existence and their unwavering commitment to guiding the multiverse through the eternal dance of evolution and change.

The Brain of the 12 Dimensions

A futuristic laboratory in Stonehenge, Salisbury Plains, Wiltshire, England. The lab is equipped with cutting-edge technology and ancient artefacts creating an atmosphere is one of intellectual curiosity and discovery.

24: Universal Economics and the Song of the Elders

Dr. Harris and her colleagues stand around a holographic display of a brain, representing the consciousness of the 12 dimensions.

Dr. Harris: "The brain of the 12 dimensions is a complex network that transcends our understanding of time and space. Each dimension interacts with the others, creating a vast, interconnected consciousness."

Professor Cohen: "Our task is to decode how perception and reality are formed within this network. It could revolutionize our understanding of the universe."

Dr. Patel: "Perception is influenced by countless variables across dimensions. If we can map these interactions, we might be able to manipulate reality itself."

Dr. Harris: "Let's begin by studying the neural pathways that link the dimensions. We need to understand the flow of information and how it shapes our perceptions."

The team dives into their research, determined to unlock the secrets of the multiversal brain.

The Rule of Fear

A secret underground bunker in Peckham, London. The room is dimly lit, with walls covered in conspiracy theories and survivalist supplies. Zam Zam and Amma find themselves in Marcus's bunker, seeking answers about the pervasive fear that seems to grip humanity.

Marcus: "Fear is the ultimate control mechanism. Those who understand it can manipulate reality to their will."

Amma: "But why is fear so powerful?"

Marcus: "It's primal. Fear triggers responses that bypass rational thought. In the 12 dimensions, fear can distort perception and create false realities."

Zam Zam: "How do we break free from the rule of fear?"

Marcus: "By understanding its origins and facing it head-on. Knowledge and courage are your weapons."

Amma: "We need to spread this understanding. People must realize that fear is an illusion that can be overcome."

24: Universal Economics and the Song of the Elders

Zam Zam: "Amma, how many times have I told you when elders are talking you youngins need to be silent. "

Amma: "Shut up, this is not a joking matter. Time and place boy, time and place."

Zam Zam: "Say no more. But seriously, we understand that fear is an illusion. Once an imagination is created, it becomes near impossible to 'unimagine' it as not 'real'. Our brains cannot tell the difference between imagined vs actual reality— it is our perception that shapes our reality, even our illusions. So to the average mind this is an impossible task."

Amma: "I hear that, but you could have said all of that without messing about."

Zam Zam: "Okay! Why you being so uptight all of a sudden, you tease me all the time… what's the matter Amma?"

Amma: "I am afraid Zam. I was just say to you guys we need to tell people that they can overcome their fears, but here am I crumbling under mine. It like I am afraid that I am always going to be afraid, if that makes sense."

Zam Zam: "It makes perfect sense Amma. We will overcome your fears together."

24: Universal Economics and the Song of the Elders

Marcus: "You two love birds are right, unraveling imaginary…"

Before Marcus could finish his statement Zam Zam and Amma speedily interjected echoing in unison: "No, No, No… We are not…absolutely not…hahahaha 'love birds' you know…that jokes."

Marcus smiles, seeing a spark of hope in their determination and undeniable love for each other.

Flash forward

Disasters – The End of All Things

A devastated cityscape in Arkansas, USA. The once-thriving city now lies in ruins, with debris scattered everywhere and an eerie silence filling the air. Dr. Carter and Officer Hernandez help Laura sift through the rubble, searching for signs of life and hope amidst the devastation.

Dr. Carter: "This disaster was caused by a dimensional rift. The barriers between realities are weakening."

Laura: "Is there any hope left? Can we rebuild?"

24: Universal Economics and the Song of the Elders

Officer Hernandez: "We must. But first, we need to understand how these rifts are formed and how to prevent them. Fill me in Dr. and please try not to talk science to me, I'm not good with the techy stuff."

Dr. Carter: "I'll try…It starts with education and awareness. People need to know that their actions have consequences beyond their immediate reality. It's fine, continuing consequences of the rifts at these point is inevitable "

Laura: "So, our future depends on how well we can learn and adapt?"

Dr. Carter: "Exactly. We must face these disasters, as we simultaneously figure out how to prevent future rifts in the aftermath."

The trio continues their work, determined to find a way to prevent further catastrophes and rebuild their world.

In Stonehenge, Dr. Harris, Professor Cohen, and Dr. Patel work to decode the brain of the multiverse, aiming to understand how perception shapes reality. exploring the intricate relationship between perception and reality across the 12 dimensions. In Peckham, Zam Zam and Amma confront the power of fear, learning that knowledge and courage can overcome its distorting effects. In

24: Universal Economics and the Song of the Elders

Arkansas, Dr. Carter, Laura, and Officer Hernandez face the aftermath of a disaster caused by a dimensional rift, realizing that understanding and adapting to these events is crucial for preventing future catastrophes. These themes of fear, disaster, and the power of perception, highlights the importance of knowledge, courage, and resilience in shaping our perceptions and reality.

Perception and Reality

The Brain of the 12 Dimensions

The Brain of the 12 Dimensions is a metaphysical construct where the consciousness of each dimension intersects. It's a place of immense mental and spiritual activity, where thoughts and perceptions shape reality.

The Rule of Fear

In the Brain of the 12 Dimensions, Elder Wariamn, Dr. Alara Tanis, High Priestess Amina, and Archivist Zara convene to discuss the pervasive influence of fear.

Elder Wariamn "Fear is a powerful force. It shapes perceptions and, consequently, realities across the dimensions."

24: Universal Economics and the Song of the Elders

Dr. Alara Tanis: "On Earth, fear often drives conflicts and divisions. We must find ways to counteract it with understanding and compassion."

High Priestess Amina: "In Nigeria, we have learned that facing our fears and understanding their roots can lead to profound healing."

Adama: "In Kenya, we teach that courage is not the absence of fear, nor the mastery of it, but the mastery of self."

High Priestess Amina: "I like that."

Archivist Zara: "The archives show that realms that have mastered themselves, overcome their fears achieved greater harmony and progress. It's andessential to address this at a fundamental level."

Disasters—the End of All Things

Earth, various disaster-stricken areas.

Dr. Alara Tanis travels to areas on Earth affected by natural and man-made disasters, observing the devastation and speaking with those affected.

24: Universal Economics and the Song of the Elders

Dr. Alara Tanis: "These disasters are a stark reminder of the fragility of our world. How we respond to them can either exacerbate the fear or foster resilience."

In Southeast China, she meets with local leaders and survivors of a recent earthquake.

Local Leader (China): "我们正在重建我们的家园和生活。团结和希望是我们的支柱。" (We are rebuilding our homes and lives. Unity and hope are our pillars.)

Survivor: "在灾难中，我们学会了珍惜每一个瞬间，并彼此依靠。" (In disaster, we have learned to cherish every moment and rely on each other.)

In Kenya, she observes efforts to combat drought and speaks with community leaders.

Local Leader (Kenya): "Tunapambana na ukame kwa kuleta suluhisho za kudumu na kushirikiana." (We are fighting drought by bringing sustainable solutions and collaborating.)

Survivor: "Umoja wetu na azimio letu ni nguvu yetu kubwa." (Our unity and determination are our greatest strengths.)

Dr. Alara Tanis: "These communities show that even in the face of disaster, the human spirit is resilient. By fostering hope and unity, we can overcome the fear that disasters bring."

24: Universal Economics and the Song of the Elders

The metaphysical Brain of the 12 Dimensions.

Back in the Brain of the 12 Dimensions, the group discusses the interplay between perception and reality.

Elder Wariamn "Our perceptions shape our realities. By changing how we perceive fear and disasters, we can transform their impact on our lives."

Dr. Alara Tanis: "Education and awareness are key. If we can teach individuals to understand and manage their fears, we can create a more stable reality."

High Priestess Amina: "In Nigeria, we use rituals and teachings to help people confront their fears. This empowers them to change their perception and, thus, their reality."

Adama: "In Kenya, storytelling is a powerful tool. Through stories, we pass down lessons of courage and resilience, shaping how future generations perceive challenges."

Archivist Zara: "The archives confirm that realms with a positive perception of reality, despite challenges, thrive. It's a testament to the power of the mind."

24: Universal Economics and the Song of the Elders

The group devises strategies to promote positive perceptions and resilience across the dimensions, aiming to create a more harmonious multiverse.

The profound impact of perception on reality in highlighted, focusing on the role of fear and how it shapes experiences across the dimensions. By drawing on the wisdom and practices of different cultures, they develop strategies to promote positive perceptions and unity, ultimately aiming to create a more stable and harmonious multiverse.

24: Universal Economics and the Song of the Elders

Song | 9

The Guardians of Cosmic Balance

The Quintessential Delusion of Hope

The Ninth Song

Balance Chamber

The Balance Chamber, a sanctum dedicated to the delicate art of maintaining cosmic equilibrium, is a place of profound stillness and order. The chamber is designed with intricate geometric patterns, symbolizing the interconnectedness of all realms. The walls are adorned with luminous glyphs that pulse with the heartbeat of the multiverse, reflecting the constant flow of energy and matter. At the centre of the chamber lies an immense, floating scale, perfectly balanced, representing the equilibrium the Elders strive to preserve.

Maintaining Cosmic Balance

The Elders play a crucial role as guardians of cosmic balance, ensuring that the multiverse remains in a state of harmony. They intervene in major cosmic events, steering the course of reality and preventing disruptions that could lead to chaos. Their pivotal interventions, and the impact of their actions on the fabric of reality, is the reason ethical considerations that guide their decisions are crucial.

24: Universal Economics and the Song of the Elders

Ibar (Ancient Paleo- Hebrew/ Phoenician Script

24: Universal Economics and the Song of the Elders

Transliteration

Aka

A na-akpiw igwai kpakpandaw n'akiw,

A na-aigyi ikai na nkainkai awriw awriw nkai akara aka.

Ikai na amamihai gyikawtara awniw, imaipiwta ngwa awriw mgbanwai.

Igbo Translation:

Eke

Ubochi Ahia Eke nke atọ

A na-akpụ ígwè kpakpando n'ọkụ,

A na-eji ike na nkenke arụ ọrụ nke akara aka.

Ike na amamihe jikọtara ọnụ,

Ịmepụta ngwá ọrụ mgbanwe.

24: Universal Economics and the Song of the Elders

English Translation:

Aka

Third Aka Market Rise

Star iron is forged in flame,

Tools of destiny are crafted with strength and precision.

Power and wisdom merge,

Creating the instruments of change.

Deliberations on the Ethics of Intervention

Elder Achichi: (observing the floating scale) "Every action we take ripples through the multiverse, altering the delicate balance we strive to maintain. Our interventions must be measured and deliberate."

Elder Alara: (adjusting a luminous glyph) "Indeed, Achichi. We hold immense power, but with it comes a profound responsibility. The ethics of our intervention are paramount. We must ensure that our actions align with the principles of harmony and justice."

24: Universal Economics and the Song of the Elders

Elder Saraphina: (contemplating the patterns on the walls) "There are times when our interventions can prevent catastrophic events. Yet, we must also respect the natural course of evolution. Intervening too often or too forcefully can stifle growth and learning."

The Elders discuss recent cosmic events and the need for intervention.

Elder Achichi: "There is a disturbance in the Gbiwriwgbiwriw Cluster. A rogue star threatens to collapse into a black hole, potentially destabilizing several nearby realms. Our intervention could avert disaster."

Elder Alara: "We must consider the broader implications. Saving these realms could prevent widespread chaos, but we also risk interfering with the natural cycles of creation and destruction."

Elder Saraphina: "We have faced similar dilemmas before. Each time, we must weigh the potential outcomes and decide whether to act or allow events to unfold naturally."

The conversation shifts to the ethical considerations of their role.

24: Universal Economics and the Song of the Elders

Elder Achichi: "Our mandate is to uphold universal principles. Yet, these principles can be challenging to interpret. What constitutes 'balance' in a situation fraught with moral complexity?"

Elder Alara: "Balance is not always about maintaining the status quo. Sometimes, it requires embracing change and allowing certain events to occur. Our task is to discern when intervention is necessary and when it is best to let things be."

Elder Saraphina: "We must also remember that our perspective is limited. We are powerful, but we are not Ama-niilai-mara (omniscient). Humility and wisdom must guide our actions."

The Elders reflect on their commitment to upholding cosmic balance.

Elder Achichi: "Our role is both a privilege and a burden. We must continually strive to act with integrity and wisdom, recognizing the profound impact of our decisions."

Elder Alara: "Let us reaffirm our commitment to the principles that guide us. May our actions always serve the greater good, even when the path is unclear."

Elder Saraphina: "And let us support one another in this journey. Together, we are stronger and wiser, capable of maintaining the balance that sustains the multiverse."

The Elders' discussions highlight the complexity of their role as guardians of cosmic balance. Their deliberations reveal the ethical dilemmas they face and their unwavering commitment to upholding universal principles. Through their careful consideration and collective wisdom, the Elders strive to maintain harmony in the multiverse, ensuring that their interventions align with the greater good and the natural flow of cosmic events.

The Difference Between Perceived and Actual Hope

A bustling street market in Southeast Kenya. Stalls are filled with colorful textiles, fresh produce, and handcrafted goods. The air is lively filled with the sounds of haggling and laughter. Mwangi and Amina are discussing the future of their community. Kariuki listens skeptically from his nearby stall.

Mwangi: "Amina, your optimism is refreshing. But hope alone won't change our situation."

Amina: "Hope is the first step. It gives us the strength to strive for a better future."

24: Universal Economics and the Song of the Elders

Kariuki: "I've seen many hopeful dreams crushed by reality. True change requires action, not just hope."

Amina: "But without hope, we wouldn't even try. It's a balance – we need both vision and effort."

Mwangi: "She's right, Kariuki. We must believe in our potential and work hard to realize it."

Kariuki sighs but nods, acknowledging the wisdom in their words.

No Way in, No Way Out

A high-security research facility in Southeast China, surrounded by thick forests and guarded by advanced technology. The facility is both a marvel of modern science and a prison for its researchers. Dr. Wang, Liang, and Yara are in a secure lab, studying a containment field that traps dimensional travelers.

Dr. Wang: "This field is designed to prevent unauthorized travel between dimensions. But it's also trapping us in our current reality."

Liang: "The true prison is not physical. It's the belief that we are limited by our circumstances."

24: Universal Economics and the Song of the Elders

Yara: "So, how do we escape this mental prison?"

Liang: "By expanding our consciousness. We must see beyond the apparent barriers and understand that our potential is limitless."

Dr. Wang: "Knowledge and perception are the keys. We need to trust our ability to transcend these constraints."

They continue their research, inspired by Liang's wisdom to seek freedom beyond the physical limitations. But can they break free from their mental prison, and even if they do, wouldn't they be exposed to invasions from other dimensional travellers?

Breaking Free from the Cycle

A serene beach in Guinea Bissau at sunrise. The sky is painted with hues of golden yellow and orange, and the sound of waves crashing creates a peaceful ambiance. Adama and Fatou watch Nia play by the water, discussing the cycles of their lives and the possibility of breaking free.

24: Universal Economics and the Song of the Elders

Adama: "We live in cycles, repeating the same patterns. Is there a way out?"

Fatou: "Breaking free requires change. We need to do things differently, think differently."

Adama: "But what if we fail?"

Fatou: "Failure is part of the journey. It's through trying and failing that we learn and grow."

Nia: *running up to them* "Look, Mama! Papa! I found a beautiful shell!"

Fatou: *smiling* "See, Adama? Beauty and hope are all around us. We just need to look for them and believe in our ability to find a new path."

Adama smiles encouraged by his family's hope and determination.

In Southeast Kenya, Mwangi, Amina, and Kariuki discuss the importance of balancing hope with action to create meaningful change, exploring the fine line between perceived and actual hope, and the challenges of breaking free from restrictive cycles. In Southeast China, Dr. Wang, Liang, and Yara face the physical and mental barriers of their high-security research facility, realizing that true freedom comes from expanding their consciousness. On a serene beach in Guinea Bissau, Adama,

24: Universal Economics and the Song of the Elders

Fatou, and their daughter Nia find inspiration in their surroundings, understanding that breaking free from life's cycles requires a blend of hope, effort, and the willingness to learn from failures, highlighting the power of hope, the importance of perception, and the courage needed to transcend limitations.

The Quintessential Delusion of Hope

Earth and Various Realms in the Multiverse

The Difference Between Perceived and Actual Hope

The focus shifts between Earth and different realms within the multiverse, exploring the concept of hope and its impact on individuals and societies.

Earth, Switzerland - CERN Laboratory

Dr. Alara Tanis and Dr. Lucas Bern walk through the bustling halls of CERN, discussing their latest findings and the role of hope in scientific research. Dr. Alara Tanis: "Hope drives us to pursue the unknown, but it must be grounded in reality to be truly effective."

24: Universal Economics and the Song of the Elders

Dr. Lucas Bern: "Absolutely. We've seen how unfounded hope can lead to disappointment and setbacks. Our research must balance optimism with rigorous methodology."

They join a video call with Dr. Mei Wang, who is in her lab in Southeast China.

Dr. Mei Wang: "我们必须找到实际与希望之间的平衡。这就是科学的真正意义。" (We must find a balance between reality and hope. This is the true essence of science.)

Dr. Lucas Bern: "Well said, Mei. Our goal is to harness hope to drive innovation while remaining anchored in what is achievable."

The team discusses their ongoing projects and how they can maintain this balance, ensuring that their work is both hopeful and realistic.

No Way in, No Way Out

Southeast Nigeria, Temple of Ahia-ka-Ala

High Priestess Amina stands at the entrance of the Temple of Ahia-ka-Ala, welcoming villagers who seek her wisdom and blessings.

24: Universal Economics and the Song of the Elders

Chidi: "Priestess Amina, I feel trapped. My hopes for a better future seem out of reach. What should I do?"

High Priestess Amina: "Chidi, hope is not just about waiting for a miracle. It's about taking steps, no matter how small, toward your dreams. Let me tell you a story from our ancestors..."

She begins to tell a story of resilience and determination, illustrating how hope, when combined with action, can lead to transformation.

High Priestess Amina: "Remember, Chidi, hope is a journey. Embrace each step and stay true to your path."

The Illusion of False Promises

Kenya, Maasai Mara

Adama and Elder Kito sit under the shade of an acacia tree, surrounded by local youths' eager to hear their wisdom.

Local Youth 1: "Elder Kito, we've heard promises of wealth and success from outsiders, but they never seem to come true. What should we believe in?"

24: Universal Economics and the Song of the Elders

Elder Kito: "Promises without substance are like clouds without rain. They can lead you astray. True hope is built on trust and actions that align with our values."

Adama: "In our community, we must rely on each other and our traditions. Real hope comes from within and from the bonds we share."

The youths nod, understanding the lesson that true hope is not about empty promises but about meaningful actions and relationships.

Hope as a Catalyst for Change

The Brain of the 12 Dimensions

Back in the Brain of the 12 Dimensions, the group discusses the concept of hope and its impact on the multiverse.

Elder Wariamn "Hope can be a powerful catalyst for change, but it must be grounded in reality to be effective."

Dr. Alara Tanis: "We've seen how false hope can lead to despair. We must foster a type of hope that empowers and inspires real action."

24: Universal Economics and the Song of the Elders

High Priestess Amina: "In Nigeria, we teach that hope is a combination of faith and effort. It's about believing in a better future while working towards it."

Adama: "In Kenya, hope is tied to our community and our connection to the land. It's about sustaining our traditions and supporting each other."

Archivist Zara: "The archives show that realms where hope is both realistic and communal tend to thrive. Let's ensure our initiatives reflect this understanding."

The group formulates strategies to promote genuine hope across the multiverse, aiming to inspire action and resilience.

The nature of hope, and the difference between perceived vs actual hope is explored. We also see the importance of grounding hope in reality and taking meaningful actions to realize it. The narrative highlights the dangers of false promises and the power of community and tradition in fostering genuine hope. By understanding and promoting realistic hope, they aim to create a more resilient and empowered multiverse.

Song | 10

Legacy and Future

12 Colours of Perception

Hall of Remembrance

The Hall of Remembrance is a solemn and reverent space, filled with the reverberations of the past. The walls are adorned with portraits of past Elders, their eyes gazing out with wisdom and serenity. Each portrait is accompanied by a glowing inscription that tells the story of their contributions to the council and the multiverse. In the centre of the hall stands a grand, circular table made of an ancient, luminescent material, around which the current Elders gather to reflect and plan for the future.

Reflecting on Legacy and Planning for the Future

The legacy of the Elders is a rich tapestry of wisdom, sacrifice, and leadership. As the current council contemplates the future, they are mindful of the lessons from their predecessors. They reflect on the past, their considerations for the continuity of leadership, and their vision for the ongoing evolution of the multiverse.

24: Universal Economics and the Song of the Elders

Ibar (Ancient Paleo-Hebrew/ Phoenician Script)

SONG 10

24: Universal Economics and the Song of the Elders

Transliteration

Ahphar

Ndagwiwriw ntiwghari iwchai na-aikpiwghai aiziawkwiw,

Ngawsipiwta nkai mkpiwriw awbi na-aigawsipiwta ihai di n'imai.

Ngyaim na-achaw nghawta,

Mpaghara aichichai na-aidiwga n'iza agyiwgyiw.

Igbo Translation

Afọ

Ubochi Ahia Afọ nke atọ

Ndagwurugwu ntụgharị uche na-ekpughe eziokwu;

Ngosipụta nke mkpụrụ obi na-egosipụta ihe dị n'ime.

Njem na-achọ nghọta,

Mpaghara echiche na-eduga n'iza ajụjụ.

24: Universal Economics and the Song of the Elders

English Translation:

Ahphar

Third Ahphar Market Rise

The valley of reflections reveals truth,

Mirrors of the soul reflect the inner self.

A journey in search of understanding,

Fields of thought lead to answers.

Continuity of Leadership and Future Vision

Elder Achichi: (gazing at the portraits) "Each of these Elders left an indelible mark on the fabric of our reality. Their legacies remind us of the weight of our responsibilities and the importance of our stewardship."

Elder Alara: (reading an inscription) "The wisdom they imparted continues to guide us. Yet, as we face new challenges, we must also innovate and adapt. Our legacy will be defined by how we balance tradition with progress."

Elder Saraphina: (placing a hand on the table) "Succession is a critical issue. We must ensure that future generations are prepared to carry the mantle

24: Universal Economics and the Song of the Elders

of leadership. This involves not only imparting knowledge but also fostering the right qualities of character and judgment."

The Elders discuss succession plans and the importance of mentorship.

Elder Achichi: "We should identify potential successors early and involve them in our deliberations. Mentorship is key. They need to understand not just the mechanics of governance, but the deeper ethical and philosophical foundations of our work."

Elder Alara: "Agreed. We must also provide them with opportunities to lead on smaller matters, gradually increasing their responsibilities. This will build their confidence and competence."

Elder Saraphina: "And we must encourage diversity in thought and background. The multiverse is vast and varied, and our council should reflect that diversity to make well-rounded decisions."

The conversation shifts to the council's vision for the future.

Elder Achichi: "What is our vision for the ongoing evolution of the multiverse? How do we see our role in guiding that evolution?"

24: Universal Economics and the Song of the Elders

Elder Alara: "We must focus on fostering balance and harmony, as always. But we also need to be proactive in addressing emerging challenges, such as technological advancements and their potential disruptions."

Elder Saraphina: "Our vision should include the promotion of interdimensional cooperation. By building stronger alliances, we can create a more resilient and united multiverse."

The Elders reflect on the importance of adaptability and foresight.

Elder Achichi: "Change is the only constant. Our ability to adapt to new circumstances while staying true to our core principles will define our success."

Elder Alara: "Foresight is essential. We must remain vigilant and anticipate future trends and challenges. This requires ongoing learning and openness to new ideas."

Elder Saraphina: "Let us commit to a future where wisdom, justice, and harmony prevail. By honoring our past and embracing the possibilities of the future, we can ensure the continued evolution and prosperity of the multiverse."

24: Universal Economics and the Song of the Elders

The Elders' reflections on legacy and future underscore the continuity of their mission. Their discussions highlight the importance of succession planning, mentorship, and a forward-thinking vision. As they navigate the complexities of leadership, the Elders remain dedicated to upholding the values that have guided their predecessors, ensuring that the council remains a strong-tower of wisdom and stability in an ever-evolving multiverse.

How Thoughts and Perceptions Create Our Vast Realities

A vibrant art studio in Enugu, Southeast Nigeria. The walls are adorned with colorful paintings and sculptures, reflecting diverse human experiences. Chinwe is working on a new painting while Amara mixes colors. Kelechi observes the artwork, intrigued by the themes and imagery.

Kelechi: "Your art captures so many emotions and perspectives. How do you decide what to paint?"

Chinwe: "My thoughts and perceptions guide me. Each piece represents a different reality shaped by my experiences and imagination."

24: Universal Economics and the Song of the Elders

Amara: "It's fascinating how our minds can create entire worlds with just a brushstroke or a thought."

Chinwe: "Our realities are as vast as our imaginations. It's all about how we see with our minds eyes, how we feel with our emotions, how we...By exploring different perspectives, we can understand the depth and diversity of human experience."

Kelechi: "It's like each painting is a portal to a different dimension, showing us the beauty and complexity of our world."

The conversation continues, exploring the profound connection between thoughts, perceptions, and reality.

Earth, Southeast Nigeria

High Priestess Amina gathers the villagers in a circle beneath a large, ancient tree. The air is thick with anticipation as she begins to speak.

High Priestess Amina: "Our thoughts and perceptions are powerful. They shape our reality more than we realize. Today, I will share a story about the 12 Colours of Perception and how our thoughts define our worlds."

She recounts the tale of the 12 Colours of Perception, each representing a unique aspect of human perception and experience. The villagers listen intently, reflecting on their own lives and communities.

Chidi: "So, Priestess, does this mean we can change our reality by changing our thoughts?"

High Priestess Amina: "Indeed, Chidi. By altering our perceptions, we can transform our experiences. It begins with embracing our inner selves. So, rather than understand I employ you to innerstand"

Biological Manipulation and Responses to Imagined Versus Real Experiences

A high-tech genetics lab in Southeast Switzerland. The lab is filled with advanced equipment and holographic displays showing DNA sequences. Dr. Müller and Lena are examining holographic DNA sequences while Johann undergoes a series of tests.

24: Universal Economics and the Song of the Elders

Dr. Müller: "Our research shows that imagined experiences can trigger biological responses almost identical to real experiences."

Lena: "It's remarkable how the brain can't always distinguish between reality and imagination."

Johann: "Does this mean we can manipulate our biology through thought alone?"

Dr. Müller: "To some extent, yes. By altering our perceptions, we can influence our physical state. It opens up new possibilities for healing and transformation."

Lena: "But we must be cautious. The line between reality and illusion is delicate, and manipulating it can have unintended consequences."

Johann: "Delicate… lines…unintended consequences…is my brain going to be okay?"

Lena laughs, "your brain is going to be just fine, lay back and relax."

They continue their research, exploring the potential and risks of biological manipulation through perception.

Switzerland, CERN Laboratory

Dr. Alara Tanis and Dr. Lucas Bern are in the genetics lab at CERN, studying the effects of biological manipulation on human perception.

Dr. Lucas Bern: "Our latest findings suggest that genetic alterations can influence how individuals perceive reality. This has profound implications for understanding the human experience."

Dr. Alara Tanis: "Yes, but it also raises ethical concerns. How do we ensure these manipulations are used responsibly and do not lead to unintended consequences?"

The research team discusses the potential benefits and risks, emphasizing the need for ethical guidelines and careful consideration.

Research Team Member: "We must tread carefully. The line between enhancement and exploitation is thin."

Dr. Alara Tanis: "Agreed. Our goal is to enhance well-being and understanding, not to create divisions or inequalities."

24: Universal Economics and the Song of the Elders

Kenya, Maasai Mara

Adama and Elder Kito lead a group of local youths on a walk through the Maasai Mara, discussing the difference between real and imagined experiences.

Local Youth 2: "Adama, how can we tell the difference between what is real and what is imagined? Sometimes our dreams feel just as real as our waking life."

Adama: "Our minds are powerful, and our imaginations can create vivid experiences. The key is to ground ourselves in our traditions and the present moment."

Elder Kito: "In our culture, we use stories and rituals to help distinguish between the two. Both have their place, but we must not let imagined fears control our reality."

The youths nod, understanding the wisdom shared by their elders. They reflect on their own experiences and how they can use this knowledge to navigate their lives.

24: Universal Economics and the Song of the Elders

Why They Hate Us?

A quiet plant-based cuisine in Somerset, UK. The cuisine has a cozy, rustic charm, with wooden tables and a fireplace in the corner. Claire and David are discussing a recent incident of discrimination. Anna joins their conversation, offering her perspective.

Claire: "I don't understand why there's so much hate and prejudice. What fuels this animosity?"

David: "Fear and ignorance, mostly. People fear what they don't understand, and that fear often turns into hate."

Anna: "It's also about power. Some people feel threatened by diversity and try to maintain control by fostering division."

Claire: "But we're all human. Why can't we see beyond our differences?"

David: "Because it's easier to hate than to understand. Understanding requires empathy and effort."

Anna: "Education and dialogue are key. We need to share our stories and experiences to break down these barriers."

24: Universal Economics and the Song of the Elders

The trio continues their conversation, determined to find ways to foster understanding and combat hatred, as Anna orders some grilled yam marinated in garlic and black pepper with lightly salted mashed avocados.

Thoughts and perceptions shape reality. Fear and uncertainty gives rise to the potential of biological manipulation by those who can, and this is the root of prejudice. It is thereby important to ground perceptions in Iwala (Divine laws in Ibar). In Enugu, Chinwe, Amara, and Kelechi discuss how art reflects the vastness of human experience and the power of imagination. In Southeast Switzerland, Dr. Müller, Lena, and Johann investigate how imagined experiences can influence biological responses, revealing both potential and risks. In Somerset, Claire, David, and Anna tackle the issue of hatred and prejudice, recognizing the role of fear and ignorance and advocating for education and empathy. Understanding the interplay between mind and body, is important for accepting, overcoming division, understanding and dismantling negative perceptions. By promoting positive perceptions with aim to create a more harmonious and inclusive multiverse.

24: Universal Economics and the Song of the Elders

Flashback

Earth, various locations

The scene shifts to various locations on Earth, where the characters simultaneously address the question of why certain groups face hatred and prejudice.

Dr. Alara Tanis (in Switzerland): "Prejudice often stems from fear and misunderstanding. By fostering education and dialogue, we can combat these negative perceptions."

High Priestess Amina (in Nigeria): "Hatred is a reflection of the hater's own insecurities and ignorance. We must respond with compassion and strength, showing that we will not be defined by their hatred."

Adama (in Kenya): "Our community stands united against prejudice. We celebrate our diversity and use it as a source of strength rather than division."

Engagements are made with communities, leading initiatives to promote understanding and unity. Through education, cultural exchange, and open dialogue, work continues to dismantle the roots of hatred.

24: Universal Economics and the Song of the Elders

Community Leader (in Nigeria): "By understanding each other's stories and experiences, we build bridges instead of walls."

Local Resident (in Switzerland): "Prejudice cannot survive in the light of knowledge and empathy. We must shine that light wherever we go."

Song | 11

Fractured Hope

Navigating Emotions

A picturesque, serene hillside in Arkansas, USA, overlooking an exuberant valley. The sun is setting, casting a golden glow over the landscape. Amaka, Nwabungwu, and Tamara sit on the hillside, discussing the future of their community and the environment.

Amaka: "Despite everything, I still believe there's hope for our planet. We can make a difference."

Nwabungwu: "Hope is vital. It's what keeps us fighting, even when the odds are against us."

Tamara: "Our emotions are powerful. They drive us to action and give us the strength to persevere."

Amara "So, we need to harness our emotions and use them to fuel our efforts."

Nwabungwu: "Exactly. Hope is just the beginning. With determination and hard work, we can achieve great things."

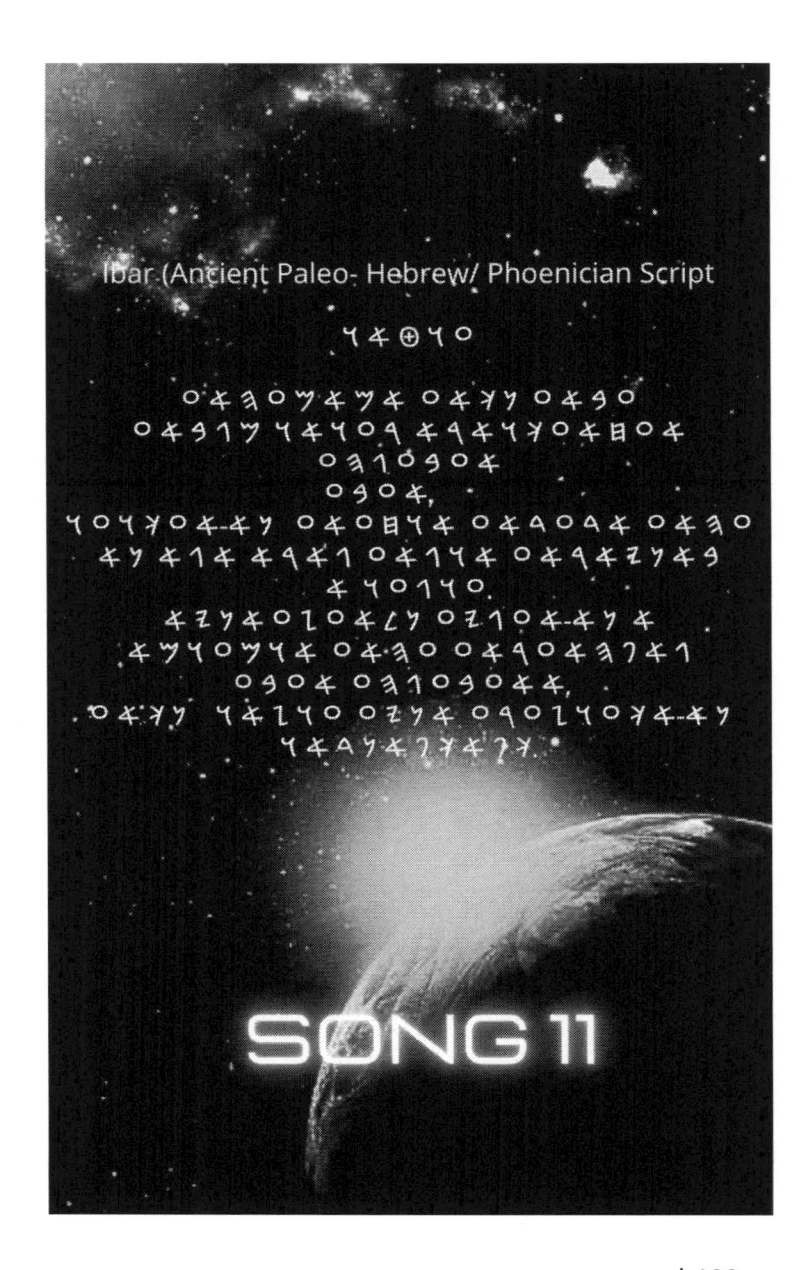

24: Universal Economics and the Song of the Elders

Ibar (Ancient Paleo- Hebrew/ Phoenician Script)

SONG 11

24: Universal Economics and the Song of the Elders

Transliteration

Iwtaw

Ibai nkai amamihai aichaikwara riwaw mgbai aibighi aibi,

Ihai adidai awchiai na-aikwiw banyairai awgai gara aga na iwgbiw a.

A na-aigyi nlaizianya gaphairai ihai awmiwma aibighi aibi,

Na-akiwziri anyi iwzaw nkai kpakpandaw.

Igbo Translation

Uto

Ahịa Igwe dị elu

Ibe nke amamihe echekwara ruo mgbe ebighị ebi,

Ihe odide ochie na-ekwu banyere oge gara aga na ugbu a.

A na-eji nlezianya gafere ihe ọmụma ebighị ebi,

Na-akụziri anyị ụzọ nke kpakpando.

24: Universal Economics and the Song of the Elders

English Translation:

<u>Uto</u>

Higher Celestial Market Rise

Pages of wisdom preserved forever,

Ancient manuscripts tell of past and present.

Eternal knowledge is carefully passed,

Teaching us the ways of the stars.

Con-Science

Advanced Research Facility in Southeast Honduras: A high-tech, bustling lab filled with cutting-edge equipment and scientists deeply engaged in their work. The atmosphere is dynamic and innovative. Dr. Martinez and his team are investigating how emotions can influence scientific outcomes, particularly in the realm of AI and data interpretation.

24: Universal Economics and the Song of the Elders

Dr. Martinez: "We've discovered that emotions can affect how AI interprets data. It's almost as if we can con the sensors by projecting certain feelings."

Sofia: "That's incredible. So, our emotions can manipulate scientific results?"

Nila: "It seems so. But this raises ethical questions. How do we ensure we're not compromising the integrity of our research?"

Dr. Martinez: "We need to find a balance. Understanding the impact of emotions can lead to breakthroughs, but we must be cautious."

Sofia: "Emotions are a double-edged sword. They can drive innovation but also introduce bias."

Nila: "Perhaps the key is to develop systems that can account for and adapt to emotional influences."

They continue their discussion, delving into the complexities of emotions and scientific manipulation.

For Better or Worse

A cozy living room in Kinshasa, Democratic Republic of the Congo. The room is filled with family photos showing the family's lives in Enugu, Southeast Nigeria, before their big

24: Universal Economics and the Song of the Elders

move to Kinshasa. The living room has comfortable furniture, and a smell of home-cooked food, exuding a sense of home and familial love.

The family gathers in the living room, discussing the ups and downs of their lives and how emotions have shaped their experiences.

Mama Nkechi: "Life has its challenges, but our emotions are what make us human. They guide us through the good times and the bad."

Obi: "Sometimes it feels like our emotions control us more than we control them."

Zuri: "But they also connect us. Love, joy, sorrow – they bring us closer together and make us stronger."

Mama Nkechi: "True. Emotions can be difficult to navigate, but they are essential to our growth and resilience."

Obi: "So, we must embrace our emotions, for better or worse, and learn from them."

Zuri: "And support each other through all the highs and lows."

24: Universal Economics and the Song of the Elders

The family shares a moment of unity, feeling the strength of their emotional bonds.

In Arkansas, Amaka, Nwabungwu, and Tamara find hope in their efforts to protect the environment, realizing that emotions are a powerful driving force. In Southeast Honduras, Dr. Martinez, Sofia, and Nila investigate how emotions can influence scientific outcomes, grappling with the ethical implications of their findings. In Kinshasa, Mama Nkechi, Obi, and Zuri reflect on how emotions shape their experiences and relationships, embracing both the joys and challenges highlighting the importance of understanding and harnessing emotions, recognizing their dual nature as both a source of strength and a potential source of bias. They learn to navigate their emotions, using them to drive positive change and foster deeper connections.

Earth and Various Realms

The narrative shifts between Earth and various realms, illustrating how emotions can be both a source of strength and a potential obstacle.

24: Universal Economics and the Song of the Elders

Further exploring their nature, their origins, their role in shaping human experience, and their impact on the multiverse.

Temple of Ahia-ka-Ala

Earth, Southeast Nigeria

In the tranquil Temple of Ahia-ka-Ala, High Priestess Amina gathers the villagers for a session on innderstanding emotions.

High Priestess Amina: "Emotions are the essence of our being. They guide us, teach us, and sometimes challenge us. But remember, no matter how dark it gets, there is always hope."

Chidi: "Priestess Amina, how do we find hope when our emotions overwhelm us?"

High Priestess Amina: "We must learn to embrace our emotions, to understand them deeply. By doing so, we find the strength to move forward. Let me share a story of our ancestors who found hope amidst despair..."

24: Universal Economics and the Song of the Elders

As she narrates the story, the villagers listen intently, drawing inspiration from their cultural heritage.

Con-Science

Switzerland, CERN Laboratory

In the high-tech environment of CERN, Dr. Alara Tanis and Dr. Lucas Bern explore the science behind emotions and their potential to be manipulated.

Dr. Alara Tanis: "Our latest research suggests that emotions can be influenced by external stimuli. But this raises ethical questions about the manipulation of emotions."

Dr. Lucas Bern: "Indeed. If we can 'con the sensors' and alter emotional states, we must consider the consequences. How do we ensure this power is used responsibly?"

The research team debates the potential applications and ethical implications, striving to

24: Universal Economics and the Song of the Elders

balance scientific advancement with moral responsibility.

Research Team Member: "We must tread carefully. Emotions are a fundamental part of the human experience. Manipulating them could have far-reaching effects."

Dr. Alara Tanis: "Our goal should be to understand emotions, not to control them. Knowledge can empower us to use emotions for positive change."

For Better or Worse

Kenya, Maasai Mara

Adama and Elder Kito sit with a group of local youths around a campfire, discussing the dual nature of emotions.

Local Youth 1: "Emotions can be so powerful. How do we harness them for good rather than letting them lead us astray?"

24: Universal Economics and the Song of the Elders

Adama: "Emotions are neither good nor bad. They are part of us, for better or worse. It's how we understand and respond to them that matters."

Elder Kito: "In our traditions, we learn to respect all emotions. Anger, joy, sorrow—they all have their place. Through balance and wisdom, we can navigate our emotional landscapes."

The youths reflect on their own experiences, learning from the wisdom of their elders about the importance of emotional intelligence.

Local Youth 2: "I see now. Emotions are like the seasons. Each has its purpose, and understanding them helps us grow."

Emotions in the Multiverse

The Brain of the 12 Dimensions

In the ethereal space of the Brain of the 12 Dimensions, the group discusses the role of emotions in shaping reality across the multiverse.

24: Universal Economics and the Song of the Elders

- Elder Wariamn: "Emotions are the threads that weave the fabric of our existence. They connect us across dimensions and define our experiences."

Dr. Elara Tanis: "Understanding emotions scientifically helps us appreciate their complexity. But we must also respect their power and unpredictability."

High Priestess Amina: "In Nigeria, we honor our emotions through rituals and stories. This cultural wisdom guides us in navigating our inner worlds."

Adama: "In Kenya, emotions are seen as a natural part of life. By embracing them, we find strength and resilience."

Archivist Zara: "The archives show that realms which embrace emotional understanding and balance tend to flourish. It's a testament to the importance of emotional intelligence."

The group formulates strategies to promote emotional understanding and resilience across the multiverse, aiming to foster harmony and growth.

24: Universal Economics and the Song of the Elders

The nature of emotions, their role in shaping human experiences and realities across the multiverse are complex. Emotions can be both a source of strength and a potential obstacle. The narrative emphasizes the importance of understanding and embracing emotions, promoting emotional intelligence, and balancing scientific advancement with ethical responsibility. By fostering emotional understanding and resilience, they aim to create a more harmonious and empowered multiverse.

Song | 1 2

Fortified by Love

The Twelfth Song in *Various Locations Worldwide*

- The twelfth song is received and decoded globally.

- The song offers a blueprint for restoring cosmic balance.

- Communities worldwide begin to implement the song's guidance.

Scientist 1: "The song provides clear steps to restore balance. We must follow them."

Spiritual Leader: "This is our chance to make things right. We must act with pure hearts."

Common Person: "We can do this. Together, we'll bring back harmony."

24: Universal Economics and the Song of the Elders

Ibar (Ancient Paleo- Hebrew/ Phoenician Script

SONG 12

24: Universal Economics and the Song of the Elders

Transliteration

<u>Agwiw</u>

Awsisi iwdaw na-aitaw nwayaw,

Aigwiw ha na-aigyikawta na ikiwkiw Di nraw.

Aikai itiwlai na-aidiwzi iwzaw,

Igyi ghawta awnawdiw anyi na mbara igwai.

Igbo Translation

<u>Agwụ</u>

Ahịa Igwe dị elu

Osisi udo na-eto nwayọ,

Egwu ha na-ejikọta na ikuku dị nro.

Eke itule na-eduzi ụzọ,

Iji ghọta ọnọdụ anyị na mbara igwe.

.

24: Universal Economics and the Song of the Elders

English Translation:

Agwu

Higher Celestial Market Rise

Trees of harmony grow quietly,

Their songs blend with the gentle breeze.

Natural balance guides the way,

To understand our place in the universe.

Fortified by Love

An ancient temple in Southeast Gambia, surrounded by dense jungle and the sounds of wildlife. The temple is a place of spiritual significance, filled with carvings and relics. The atmosphere is serene and contemplative. Abena, Kwame, and Nia sit in the temple, discussing the power of love and its ability to break cycles of negativity.

Abena: "Love is the most powerful force in the universe. It can break the hardest chains and heal the deepest wounds."

24: Universal Economics and the Song of the Elders

Kwame: "But love is also vulnerable. How do we protect it and use it to break free from the cycles that trap us?"

Abena: "By nurturing it within ourselves and sharing it with others. Love must be cultivated and allowed to grow."

Nia: "So, love is like a seed. It needs care and attention to flourish."

Abena: "Exactly. And once it takes root, it can transform our lives and the lives of those around us."

The conversation continues, with Kwame and Nia speaking endlessly about love, but what does love have to do with it? What is the cost of love?

Love will Cost You an Arm and a Leg

A bustling hospital in Kinshasa, Democratic Republic of the Congo. The hospital is crowded, with patients and medical staff moving through the halls. The atmosphere is one of urgency and care. Dr. Mbemba checks on Dani's progress, while Marta stays by his side, reflecting on the sacrifices they've made for love.

Tai-Zamarai Yasharahyalah | 208

24: Universal Economics and the Song of the Elders

Dr. Mbemba: "Dani, you're making great progress. With time and care, you'll recover fully."

Dani: "Thank you, doctor. I couldn't have done it without Marta's support."

Marta: "Love isn't easy. It demands sacrifices, sometimes more than we think we can give."

Dr. Mbemba: "But those sacrifices are what make love so powerful. It's through giving that we fulfil that sense of divine purpose and a higher calling."

Dani: "Love has cost us so much, but it's also given us everything."

Marta: "We've faced so many challenges, but we've done it together. That's what matters."

The three share a moment of understanding, recognizing the true value and cost of love.

Try, Try, and Try Again

A crowded dynamic and vibrant marketplace in Southeast China, filled with the sounds of vendors calling out and the smell of street food. The atmosphere is lively and energetic. Wei and Li Mei are discussing their latest business

24: Universal Economics and the Song of the Elders

venture, while Chen offers advice based on his years of experience.

Wei: "We've faced so many setbacks, Li Mei. I'm starting to lose hope."

Li Mei: "We can't give up now. We've come too far."

Chen: "Success rarely comes on the first try. You must be willing to fail and try again. It's persistence that pays off."

Wei: "But how do we keep going when it feels like everything is against us?"

Chen: "By believing in your vision and supporting each other. You've got a good idea; you just need to keep refining it."

Li Mei: "Chen's right. We've learned from our mistakes. Let's use that knowledge to move forward."

Wei nods, feeling a renewed sense of determination and the strength to try again.

24: Universal Economics and the Song of the Elders

In Southeast Gambia, Abena, Kwame, and Nia discuss how love can transform lives and provide the strength to overcome challenges. In Kinshasa, Dr. Mbemba, Daniel, and Marta reflect on the sacrifices love demands and how it fortifies them through difficult times. In Southeast China, Wei, Li Mei, and Chen emphasize the importance of persistence and learning from failure to achieve success. Highlighting the power of love and resilience in breaking free from cycles of negativity and failure.

©B3.FR33 from the Cycle

Earth and Various Realms

B3.FR33 from destructive cycles, both personal and cosmic. The focus is on love as a transformative force and the determination required to change one's destiny.

24: Universal Economics and the Song of the Elders

Earth, Southeast Nigeria - Temple of Ahia-ka-Ala

High Priestess Amina stands at the centre of the Temple of Ahia-ka-Ala, surrounded by villagers. The air is filled with the scent of frankincense & myrrh and the sound of rhythmic drumming.

High Priestess Amina: "Love is the most powerful force in the universe. It can fortify us against any challenge and help us break free from the cycles that bind us."

Chidi: "Priestess, how do we harness this power of love in our daily lives?"

High Priestess Amina: "Through acts of kindness, compassion, and innderstanding. Love is not just a feeling but a series of actions. Let me tell you about the ancient ritual of Ebe N'elu, a practice that strengthens love within our community..."

She narrates the story of Ebe N'elu, a ritual where villagers' express gratitude and support for one another, fortifying their bonds of love and unity.

High Priestess Amina: "Remember, Chidi, love is a choice we make every day. By choosing love, we can overcome any obstacle."

Tai-Zamarai Yasharahyalah | 212

24: Universal Economics and the Song of the Elders

Love Will Cost You an Arm and a Leg

Switzerland, CERN Laboratory

In the sleek, high-tech environment of CERN, Dr. Alara Tanis and Dr. Lucas Bern discuss the sacrifices required for breakthroughs in their research.

Dr. Lucas Bern: "Alara, we've made significant progress, but it's come at a great cost. We've invested countless hours, and the pressure is immense."

Dr. Alara Tanis: "True, Lucas. Love for our work drives us, but it demands sacrifices. We must remember why we started and let that passion sustain us."

The team reflects on the personal and professional sacrifices they've made for their love of science, recognizing that their dedication can lead to transformative discoveries. But the love for one thing can lead to the detriment of another.

Research Team Member: "Our love for knowledge and progress is what fuels us. It's a challenging journey, but one worth every sacrifice."

24: Universal Economics and the Song of the Elders

Dr. Alara Tanis: "Indeed. Love pushes us to go beyond our limits and achieve the extraordinary."

Try, Try, and Try Again

Kenya, Maasai Mara

Adama and Elder Kito stand on the open plains of the Maasai Mara, addressing a group of local youths about the importance of perseverance.

Local Youth 1: "Adama, we've faced so many setbacks. How do we find the strength to keep going?"

Adama: "Perseverance is the key. No matter how many times we fail, we must try again. Each effort brings us closer to success."

Elder Kito: "In our culture, we say, 'Enda mbele, hata kama unaanguka,' which means 'Keep moving forward, even if you fall.' Let me tell you the story of the great hunter, Simba, who never gave up...''

Elder Kito narrates the story of Shalah, a legendary warrior who faced countless challenges but always persevered, ultimately achieving his goals.

24: Universal Economics and the Song of the Elders

Adama: "Remember, every failure is a lesson. By trying again and again, we build resilience and pave the way for future success."

Local Youth 2: "We will keep this wisdom in our hearts and continue to strive for our dreams."

Breaking Free in the Multiverse

The Brain of the 12 Dimensions

In the ethereal space of the Brain of the 12 Dimensions, the group discusses the process of breaking free from destructive cycles and the role of love and perseverance.

Elder Wariamn: "Throughout the multiverse, we see patterns of stagnation and repetition. To break free, we must embrace learn to rest in love and persevere."

Dr. Alara Tanis: "In science, we've learned that breakthroughs come from relentless pursuit and passion. Love for our work drives us to overcome obstacles."

High Priestess Amina: "In Nigeria, we teach that love and community are our greatest strengths. We

24: Universal Economics and the Song of the Elders

evolve when we persevere to becoming one. By supporting each other, we can transcend any cycle."

Adama: "In Kenya, we honor the spirit of perseverance. By trying again and again, we build the resilience needed to achieve our goals. It's a Spirit you know, Work."

All nod in acknowledgement to Adama.

Archivist Zara: "The archives show that realms which embody these principles thrive. Love and perseverance are universal keys to transformation."

The group formulates strategies to promote these values across the multiverse, aiming to inspire individuals and societies to ©B3.FR33 from their limitations and achieve their full potential.

The journey of breaking free from destructive cycles through the transformative power of love and perseverance fortifies individuals and communities. Sacrifices and dedication are required to achieve meaningful change. By embracing these values, individuals and communities can overcome any obstacles and transform their realities, inspiring a more empowered and dynamic multiverse.

24: Universal Economics and the Song of the Elders

Song | 13

The End of Believing...

Exploring the Broader Spectrum of Light

The Thirteenth Song

The mystical Stonehenge on Salisbury Plains, Wiltshire, England. An ancient and mystical site with towering stones. The ancient stones cast long shadows in the twilight, and the air is filled with a sense of history and mystery. Alana, Thomas, and Lila stand among the stones of Stonehenge, discussing the mysteries of the universe and the limits of belief.

Alana: "Light is more than what we see with our eyes. There are spectrums beyond our perception, filled with untapped potential."

Thomas: "Just like the past holds secrets yet to be discovered, the universe holds knowledge beyond our current understanding."

Lila: "So, believing in what we can't see is just as important as believing in what we can?"

Alana: "Exactly. Our understanding is limited by our perceptions. By exploring broader spectrums, we can fine tune our beliefs into profound knowledge."

Thomas: "History teaches us that belief shapes reality. The more we learn, the more our beliefs evolve."

Lila looks at the stones, feeling inspired by the infinite possibilities beyond her current understanding.

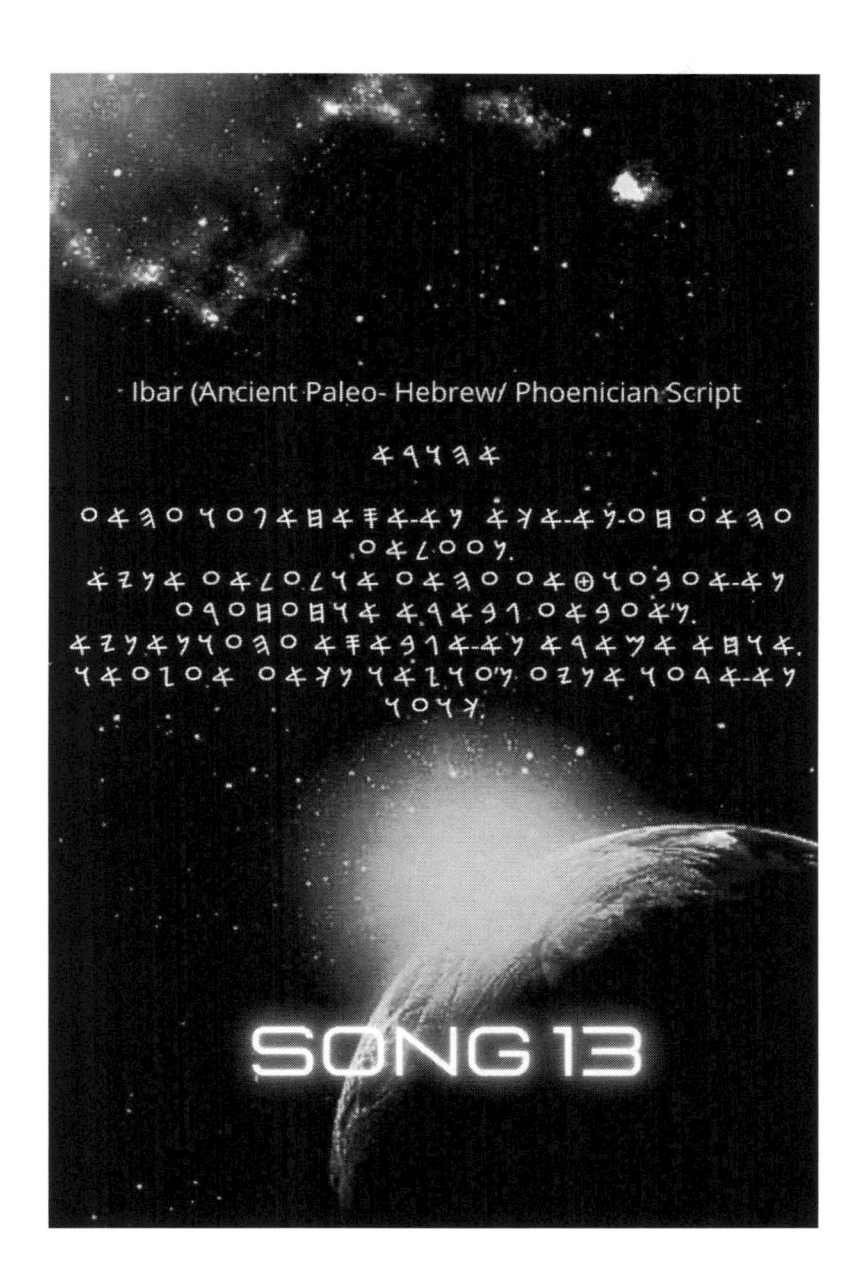

24: Universal Economics and the Song of the Elders

24: Universal Economics and the Song of the Elders

Transliteration

Ahwra

Ihai Chi-na-Aka na-asachapiw ihai niilai.

Na-aibiwtai ihai awlilai anya n'aibai gbara awchichiri.

Awcha amara na-agbasa ihiwnanya.

Na-aidiw anyi n'iwzaw nkai aiziawkwiw.

Igbo Translation

Ọra

Ahịa Igwe dị elu

Ìhè Chineke na-asachapụ ihe niile.

Na-ebute ìhè olile anya n'ebe gbara ọchịchịrị.

Ọcha amara na-agbasa ịhụnanya.

Na-edu anyị n'ụzọ nke eziokwu.

24: Universal Economics and the Song of the Elders

English Translation

Aura

Higher Celestial Market Rise

Divine light washes over all,

Bringing hope's illumination to dark places.

A glow of grace spreads love,

Guiding us on the path of truth.

The Intergalactic Saviors

High-Tech Space Station Orbiting Earth: A state-of-the-art space station with advanced technology and a panoramic view of Earth. The atmosphere is one of urgency and purpose. Captain Farah, Dr. Khan, and Lieutenant Chawan discuss their mission to save the universe from an impending threat, reflecting on the end of belief and the beginning of action.

Captain Farah: "Belief has brought us this far, but now it's time for action. We have the technology and the knowledge to make a difference."

24: Universal Economics and the Song of the Elders

Dr. Khan: "Our mission is to preserve life and ensure the survival of our species. It's a monumental task, we believe unequivocally in our capabilities, so, we must maintain the same energy in our efforts."

Lieutenant Chawan: "The universe depends on us. We need to move beyond belief and execute our plans with precision and determination."

Captain Farah: "Precision…mmm, that's the one. We've trained for this. Every challenge we've faced has prepared us for this moment. Let's show the universe what we're capable of."

They prepare for their mission, feeling the weight of their responsibility and the strength of their conviction.

Evolution and Devolution

Futuristic Laboratory in Arkansas: A cutting-edge lab filled with advanced equipment and researchers conducting experiments on evolution and devolution. The atmosphere is one of scientific curiosity and discovery. Dr. Johnson, Iwah, and Maya discuss the implications of their research on evolution and devolution, considering the end of certain beliefs and the rise of new understandings.

24: Universal Economics and the Song of the Elders

Dr. Johnson: "Our research shows that evolution is not a linear path. There are instances of devolution, where species revert to more primitive states."

Iwah: "It challenges everything we thought we knew. If species can devolve, what does that mean for our future?"

Maya: "It means we need to adapt our beliefs and be open to new possibilities. Evolution and devolution are part of a larger, more complex system."

Dr. Johnson: "Exactly. Our understanding must evolve with our discoveries. The end of one belief is the beginning of another."

Iwah: "So, we must remain curious and adaptable, always ready to embrace new knowledge."

They continue their research, feeling a sense of wonder and excitement for the future of their field.

At Stonehenge, Alana, Thomas, and Lila discuss the importance of exploring broader spectrums of light and the evolution of belief bringing an end of certain beliefs and giving rise to new understandings through unique experiences and settings On a high-tech space station, Captain Farah, Dr. Khan, and Lieutenant Chawan prepare for a mission to save the universe, moving beyond

24: Universal Economics and the Song of the Elders

belief to action. In a futuristic lab in Arkansas, Dr. Johnson, Iwah, and Maya grapple with the implications of evolution and devolution, recognizing the need to adapt their beliefs to new discoveries. This dynamic nature of belief and understanding, highlights the importance of curiosity, action, and adaptability in the face of new knowledge and challenges.

24: Universal Economics and the Song of the Elders

Song | 14

Creating a Balance

Combining Forces

The Fourteenth Song

CERN, Switzerland

- The fourteenth song is received, revealing the crucial steps to restore balance.

- The scientists at CERN understand their crucial role in the restoration process.

- The song's power inspires global hope and action.

Jean-Luc: "This song is the key. We must implement its guidance immediately."

Mei: "The world is counting on us. We must act with purity and purpose."

Alara: "Together, we can make this right. Let's restore the balance."

24: Universal Economics and the Song of the Elders

Tai-Zamarai Yasharahyalah | 226

24: Universal Economics and the Song of the Elders

Transliteration

<u>Ngwiw</u>

Awshimiri nkai ndiw na-agba nwayawaw nwayawaw.

Ikai giwgharia nkai mmalitai awhiwriw.

Mbailata awgai na-aigyiwpiwta iwgbiw a,

Na-aichaitara anyi mkpa nkai awgai aw biwla.

Igbo Translation

<u>Ngwu</u>

Ahịa Igwe dị elu

Osimiri nke ndụ na-agba nwayọọ nwayọọ.

Ike gụgharia nke mmalite ọhụrụ.

Mbelata oge na-ejupụta ugbu a,

Na-echetara anyị mkpa nke oge ọ bụla.

24: Universal Economics and the Song of the Elders

English Translation:

Ngwu

Higher Celestial Market Rise

The river of life flows gently,

Streaming energy of new beginnings.

Drops of time fill the current,

Reminding us of the importance of every moment.

Uniting Forces

Global Setting

- *Global leaders unite with scientists and spiritual leaders to restore balance.*

- *Coordinated efforts begin to reverse the damage done.*

- *The power of the songs brings hope and unity.*

Global Leader 1: "We must work together. Our survival depends on it."

Alara: "The songs have shown us the way. Let's follow their guidance."

Amina: "With unity and pure intentions, we can restore the balance."

Combing Forces

The ancient ruins of Petra, Jordan. The towering sandstone structures glow under the setting sun, creating a breathtaking and serene environment filled with historical significance. Dr. Ala-Shalah, Nnam, and Nadine sit among the ruins of Petra, discussing the importance of combining forces and knowledge from different disciplines.

Dr. Ala-Shalah: "Petra is a testament to the incredible achievements of ancient civilizations. By combining our knowledge, we can unlock its mysteries."

Nnam: "It's not just about the past. Understanding these ruins can help us build a better future."

Nadine: "We need to balance our reverence for history with our drive for innovation. Combining our forces is the key."

24: Universal Economics and the Song of the Elders

Dr. Ala-Shalah: "Working together, we can achieve a deeper understanding and create a more balanced approach to our research and discoveries."

The conversation continues, with the trio feeling inspired by the collaborative potential of their diverse expertise.

Developing a Balanced Mindset Toward Money and Life

A bustling financial district in New York City. Skyscrapers loom overhead, and the streets are filled with people rushing to and from work with a vibrant energy reflecting the fast-paced financial world. Alex, Jasmine, and Athan meet in a café in the heart of the financial district, discussing the importance of balancing financial success with personal fulfillment.

Alex: "Money is a tool, but it shouldn't dominate our lives. We need to find a balance."

Jasmine: "You know how it is, it's hard when the pressure to succeed is so high. How do we stay grounded?"

24: Universal Economics and the Song of the Elders

Athan: "By developing a balanced mindset. Focus on your goals, but also on your well-being and relationships."

Jasmine: I wish it were that simple, my husband drives me nuts!"

Alex: "Financial success is important, but it's not everything. True wealth comes from a balanced life."

Jasmine: "So, it's about aligning our financial goals with our personal values and happiness? So things just can't be fixed, chasing the bag is what I know to do…relationships are compli…messy is the word I was looking for."

Athan: "You are right, balance is the key to sustainable success and fulfilment, sounds to me you are ready to give up on your relationship. You are going to regret it in your old age when you alone with 'the bag' and a bunch of cats!"

They all laugh hysterically and continue their discussion, on the importance of having and maintaining balance in their approach to money and life.

Flash-forward

Awala—A New Sustainable Future

A Harmony of Multiverses

A futuristic city named *Awala*, located in an undisclosed region. The city is a model of sustainability and technological innovation, featuring green spaces, advanced infrastructure, and a harmonious blend of nature and technology. Mila, Yanah, and Arla stand on a rooftop garden overlooking the city, discussing the vision and implementation of Awala as a harmonious and sustainable future.

Mila: "Awala represents our dream of a sustainable future. Every aspect of the city is designed to promote balance and harmony."

Yanah: "We've integrated green technology and sustainable practices to create a self-sufficient environment."

Arla: "Our technology fosters connectivity and efficiency, allowing us to live in harmony with the environment."

Mila: "Awala is not just a city; it's a blueprint for the future. It shows what we can achieve when we prioritize balance and sustainability."

24: Universal Economics and the Song of the Elders

Yanah: "We've created a paradise that integrates the best of human innovation and natural beauty."

Arla: "And it's a testament to the power of collective effort and vision."

The group looks out over the city, feeling proud of their achievements and hopeful for the future.

At the ancient ruins of Petra, Dr. Ala-Shalah, Nnam, and Nadine discuss the importance of combining forces and knowledge from different disciplines to unlock historical mysteries and build a better future. In New York City's financial district, Alex, Jasmine, and Athan emphasize the need to balance financial success with personal fulfillment and well-being. In the futuristic city of Awala, Mila, Yanah, and Arla showcase a vision of a sustainable and harmonious future, demonstrating the power of balance in creating a paradise that centres human innovation at the heart of Iwala (Natures Laws) Nature is beautiful, and in aligning ourselves with nature, we achieve holistic success, fulfilment, and natural balance. Awala is a testament to collaboration and sustainable practices, that culminate a collective vision of peace, prosperity and reverence for all of natures creation.

24: Universal Economics and the Song of the Elders

Song | 15

Global Effort for Restoration

The Fifteenth Song

Various locations worldwide

- Efforts to restore balance are intensified globally.

- Communities work together, inspired by the songs.

- Hope and unity bring significant progress.

Scientist 1: "We're making progress. The songs are guiding us well."

Spiritual Leader: "With every action, we restore a part of the balance."

Common Person: "We can feel the change. Let's keep going."

24: Universal Economics and the Song of the Elders

Tai-Zamarai Yasharahyalah | 235

24: Universal Economics and the Song of the Elders

Transliteration

<u>Ala Igwai</u>

Ailiwigwai nkai ainwaighi ngwiwcha na-agbati aibai di anya.

Kpakpandaw na-aigbiwkai aigbiwkai na ngyaim na-adighi agwiw agwiw.

Awkirikiri idi adi na-adighi agwiw agwiw,

Na-akpali n'imai anyi awchichaw Inyawcha.

Igbo Translation

<u>Ala Igwe</u>

Ahịa Igwe dị elu

Eluigwe nke enweghị ngwụcha na-agbatị ebe dị anya.

Kpakpando na-egbuke egbuke na njem na-adịghị agwụ agwụ.

Okirikiri ịdị adị na-adịghị agwụ agwụ,

Na-akpali n'ime anyị ọchịchọ inyocha.

24: Universal Economics and the Song of the Elders

English Translation:

Awala (Heavens)

Higher Celestial Market Rise

Skies of infinity stretch afar,

Stars sparkle in an endless journey.

Circles of existence never-ending,

Inspire in us the desire to explore.

Uncharted Spaces

Switzerland, CERN Laboratory and Nigeria

Dr. Ayomide Ibrahim

Ayomide grew up in Lagos, Nigeria, in a family deeply rooted in Yoruba traditions. Her parents were educators, and her grandmother a respected priestess who taught her the ways of their ancestors.

Ayomide walks through a bustling Nigerian market, interacting with locals.

24: Universal Economics and the Song of the Elders

Ayomide (in Yoruba): "Ẹ kuulé, báwo ni o ṣe wa?" (Greetings, how are you?)

Local Vendor (in Yoruba): "Adúpe, ẹ̀bùn ríre l'áti odọ Olọ́run." *(Thank you, we are blessed by the gifts of the Supreme one.)

She later joins a village council meeting, emphasizing the importance of preserving their cultural heritage while advancing scientifically.

Ayomide: "Our traditions hold the wisdom of generations. They guide us even as we embrace modernity."

Dr. Nyah Kimani

Nyah grew up in Nairobi, Kenya, in a close-knit family. Her father was a botanist, and her mother an artist, instilling in her a love for both science and culture.

Nyah speaks with her mentor at the ancient temple, learning about her spiritual duties.

Mentor (in Swahili): "Nyah, kumbuka, hekima ya kale ni mwanga wa leo." (Nyah, remember, the wisdom of the ancients is the light of today.)

24: Universal Economics and the Song of the Elders

Nyah reflects on her dual path of science and spirituality.

Nyah: "I am honored to walk this path, merging the old with the new to find deeper truths."

Nyah Kimani's love life in the context of her journey:

Love and Relationships

Nairobi, Kenya

Nyah Kimani meets Wanjiru, a dedicated environmental activist who shares her passion for sustainable development and cultural preservation.

Nyah: "Wanjiru, ũhenia wa kũmenya arume rwa thĩ mũthi ni wa kũcokeria. Nĩmũhata ũmenya ũkĩona na gũcokia mĩaka na mĩhanda ũciara."

"Wanjiru, your dedication to our land is inspiring. I admire how you bring communities together for environmental causes."

Wanjiru: "Na we, Nyah, ũngĩndani wa gũkũrĩria ũgĩkũyũ na rũthiĩ wa ũniversitii ni wa kũhuiniria. Niwĩtũka mũhato ũguo wa ciana cia ũmenya."

24: Universal Economics and the Song of the Elders

"And you, Nyah, your blend of tradition and science is remarkable. You bring a unique perspective to our work."

Nyah: "Nĩgatonga kũria ngũgĩ, Wanjiru. Twimenya rũmwe rũriri wa ngũgĩrĩ mũthoni wa rũthiĩ kũhĩrĩa rũthiĩ."

"I feel a deep connection with you, Wanjiru. We share a vision for a sustainable future for our people."

Wanjiru: "Twihurire mũkũmenya kũrĩtia njira cia itũme, Nyah. Na mũrata na ũgũkinyana, ũrĩaũtũka kũrĩrĩria."

"Let's work together to make our dreams a reality, Nyah. With love and determination, we can achieve anything."

Nyah: "Ngwenda kũmenya kũmũka no rũmwe, Wanjiru. Na ũmenya mũtũ mũrata nĩmenya atĩ tũmũhote nyũmba."

"I look forward to building our future together, Wanjiru. Side by side, I know we can create lasting change."

Argument for Religion

The outskirts of Enugu, around Priestess Amina's temple is a serene and sacred place, surrounded by lush greenery and ancient trees. The air is thick with the scent of blooming flowers and the sounds of nature. Birds sing, leaves rustle in the gentle breeze, and the distant sound of a flowing stream adds to the tranquil atmosphere. Villagers and visitors from nearby towns pass by, some stopping to offer their respects, others engaging in quiet conversations. The temple is a blend of traditional Igbo architecture and sacred symbols, exuding an aura of ancient wisdom and spiritual power.

The Temple Grounds

The temple grounds are bustling with activity. Villagers are busy with their daily chores, children play nearby, and elders sit under the shade of the trees, discussing various matters. In the midst of this vibrant scene, a small area has been set up for a public debate. A large tree provides shade, and wooden benches have been arranged for the audience. The atmosphere is one of anticipation and curiosity.

24: Universal Economics and the Song of the Elders

Inner Dialogue of the Initiate (a young man from a nearby village): "This debate will be interesting. Priestess Amina always speaks with such wisdom, but the Christian preacher is very passionate. It's important to hear both sides, especially as our community changes and grows."

The Debate Begins

Christian: "There is only one God and only one way to life. The Bible provides us with the truth, the path to eternal salvation."

Priestess Amina: "The Bible and other religious texts are edited and manipulated by men, based on social engineering, the construct, and various interpretations and community standards including their biases. Viewing them as wrong or right is irrelevant, as it is intended to serve as a guide to usher the collective within the intended community it is created for to enable them to fulfill that community's standards of morality, social and economic predictability, general ways of living amongst each other and amongst other communities. The problem comes when religion imposes these standards on other communities, claiming to be supreme, thereby diminishing other communities' ways of life."

Christian: "There is only one god and only one way to life."

24: Universal Economics and the Song of the Elders

Priestess Amina: "But who…or what is god? Without your indoctrination and programming, you would have no context to this ideology you propose. You have been indoctrinated from an infant to call on god. Many cultures refer to the Source of Life by various names and terms based on the syntax of their language systems and their fundamental value systems passed on through generations."

Christian: "All ways seem right, but the end is destruction and eternal damnation. Hell is a real thing, and only through Jesus can one have eternal life. Look at this electronic billboard as it changes images; someone from a primitive part of the world might think it is an alien. So we have to teach them the truth that it is in fact a billboard and show them the way to use it."

Priestess Amina: "I am glad you chose that analogy because it emphasizes the cultural biases of most religions, if not all. Just because I am from what you refer to as a 'primitive' part of the world, and do not utilize or have knowledge of a digital billboard and other communication technology does not mean my community is less advanced and lacks its own systems of communication within its community. Your world perspective is not the only perspective, and indeed it is an alien in other world views!

"Imagine a wild cat immersed in nature viewing that billboard. It is indeed an alien to the overall ways and stayed living of the wild cat communities.

24: Universal Economics and the Song of the Elders

But I know what you are thinking, but we are humans and are superior to animals—are we? Look at all the harm we have caused to the planet; I doubt from a universal perspective we are being celebrated for our 'modern advancements'."

"Your religions are just extended systems of oppression that keep the people (who you view as primitive) docile and sedated whilst we ignore and or are ignorant to the weighted matters like social, economic, and environmental injustices. We ignore the underlying emergencies such as the need for DNA regeneration and repair from all the energetic, biological, and environmental pollutions. A universal feedback loop is required and people need to be more energetically conservative and choose wisely not to invest their time in oppressive systems. Religion as a process produces ignorant people as a product."

Inner Dialogue of the Initiate: "Priestess Amina is going in! She makes a compelling point. I've never thought about religion as a form of social engineering before. It makes me wonder how much of my own beliefs are influenced by the culture I was raised in. This debate is opening my eyes to the complexities of faith and cultural identity."

24: Universal Economics and the Song of the Elders

The Audience Reacts

The crowd murmurs, some nodding in agreement with the Priestess, others shaking their heads in disagreement. A few villagers exchange heated whispers, reflecting the tension in the air.

Passerby 1 (a villager): "Ọ dị ezigbo mkpa na anyị na-agụ na ihe dị iche iche. Ọtụtụ ihe anyị na-eche na ọ bụ eziokwu, ma anyị anaghị aghọta ọdịiche dị na ha."

"It is very important that we explore other perspectives. There are many things we've been made to think are true, but we are not able to distinguish what is truth from lies and the difference between them."

Passerby 2 (another villager): "Ma okwukwe bụ ihe onwe onye. Ọ na-enye ndị mmadụ olileanya na ebumnuche. Ewezuga ya, gịnị ka anyị nwere?"

"But faith is a personal thing. It gives people hope and purpose. Without it, what do we have?"

Passerby 3 (an elder): "Mkparịta ụka a dị mkpa. Ịghọta echiche dị iche iche dị mkpa maka uto uche na mmụọ n'ezie."

"This discussion is important. Understanding different perspectives is important for true mental and spiritual growth."

24: Universal Economics and the Song of the Elders

Inner Dialogue of the Initiate: "It's fascinating to see how divided everyone is. Faith and belief are so personal yet so universally debated. Maybe the key is not in finding one ultimate truth, but in understanding and respecting the diversity of truths that exist."

The Resolution

Christian: "I understand your perspective, Priestess Amina, but faith in Jesus is what brings me peace and purpose. I believe it can do the same for others."

Priestess Amina: "And I respect your faith, Christian. But remember, true wisdom comes from understanding that every path has its value and every belief its place. Let us learn from each other rather than impose our will."

The crowd begins to disperse, some continuing their discussions in smaller groups, others heading back to their homes. The air is still charged with the energy of the debate, but there is a sense of mutual respect and a willingness to understand different perspectives.

24: Universal Economics and the Song of the Elders

Inner Dialogue of the Initiate: "This debate has given me so much to think about. Maybe the real journey isn't about finding the one true path, but about exploring and understanding the many paths that exist. Respect, empathy, and open-mindedness—these are the keys to true enlightenment."

As the Initiate leaves the temple grounds, he feels a newfound sense of purpose and curiosity. The teachings of Priestess Amina about balance and understanding resonate deeply within him, guiding his steps toward a more enlightened future.

24: Universal Economics and the Song of the Elders

Song | 16

Song's Guidance

The sixteenth Song

Nigerian village, sacred grove

- *Amina receives the sixteenth song, providing crucial guidance.*

- *The villagers follow the song's steps, contributing to global efforts.*

- *The power of the song brings renewed hope and determination.*

Amina: "This song is our guide. Let's follow it with pure hearts."

Initiate 1: "We're ready, Priestess. We'll do whatever it takes."

Villager: "With this song, we can make a real difference."

24: Universal Economics and the Song of the Elders

Ibar (Ancient Paleo- Hebrew/ Phoenician Script)

SONG 16

24: Universal Economics and the Song of the Elders

Transliteration

Iwala

Iwlaw Nziwkaw nkai idi n'awtiw na-achikawta ihai niilai.

Awbi na mkpiwriw awbi gyikawaw na aigwiw.

Ngyikaw ihiwnanya na awmiikaw,

Na-aichaitara anyi na anyi biw awtiw.

Igbo Translation

Iwụ ala

Ahịa Igwe dị elu

Ụlọ Nzukọ nke ịdị n'otu na-achịkọta ihe niile.

Obi na mkpụrụ obi jikọọ na egwu.

Njikọ ịhụnanya na ọmịiko,

Na-echetara anyị na anyị bụ otu.

24: Universal Economics and the Song of the Elders

English Translation:

Universal Law of Onneness

Higher Celestial Market Rise

The hall of unity brings all together,

Hearts and souls connect in song.

A bond of love and compassion,

Reminding us that we are one.

---

12 Realities, 12 Possibilities

Switzerland, CERN Laboratory and Kenya

Dr. Carlos Mendoza

Carlos hails from Rio de Janeiro, Brazil, where he grew up surrounded by vibrant culture and music. His parents were engineers, sparking his interest in technology from a young age. Carlos works on a complex engineering project at CERN, discussing challenges with Jean-Luc.

24: Universal Economics and the Song of the Elders

Carlos: "Every problem has a solution. It's just a matter of finding the right perspective."

Dr. Hiroshi Nakamura:

Hiroshi grew up in Kyoto, Japan, steeped in the traditions of Zen Buddhism. His parents were scientists, encouraging his fascination with the stars and the fundamental questions of existence.

Hiroshi practices meditation, contemplating their recent findings.

Hiroshi (in Japanese): "宇宙の本質は私たちの理解を超えている。それを解き明かすのは、私たちの使命だ。" *(The essence of the universe is beyond our understanding. It is our mission to unravel it.)

Dr. Anya Petrov

Anya was raised in Moscow, Russia, in a family of mathematicians and philosophers. Her rigorous upbringing and love for numbers shaped her analytical mind.

Anya analyzes complex equations, engaging in a spirited debate with Mei Wang.

Anya: "Mathematics is the language of the universe. Through it, we can unlock its deepest secrets."

24: Universal Economics and the Song of the Elders

The Mechanics of the Universe and Creation

Switzerland, CERN Laboratory and Brazil

Dr. Ayomide Ibrahim

Mide's spiritual beliefs are deeply rooted in Yoruba cosmology, which sees the universe as a balanced interplay of forces.

Ayomide explains her research on ancient symbols to a group of students in Nigeria.

Ayomide: "These symbols are not just art; they are keys to understanding the universe and our place within it."

Dr. Nyah Kimani

Nyah's spirituality is a blend of traditional African beliefs and modern science, seeing the two as complementary.

Nyah leads a ritual at the temple, combining scientific knowledge with spiritual practices.

Nyah: "Science and spirituality are two sides of the same coin. Together, they reveal the full picture."

24: Universal Economics and the Song of the Elders

Dr. Carlos Mendoza:

Carlos finds spirituality in the rhythms of nature and the interconnectedness of all things, influenced by indigenous Brazilian philosophies.

Carlos shares a quiet moment with Jean-Luc, reflecting on their journey.

Carlos: "Life is a web of connections. Our work here is part of that greater tapestry."

Dr. Hiroshi Nakamura

Hiroshi integrates Zen Buddhist principles into his scientific work, seeking harmony and balance.

Hiroshi leads a meditation session for his colleagues at CERN.

Hiroshi: "In stillness, we find clarity. In clarity, we find answers."

Dr. Anya Petrov:

Anya's beliefs are shaped by Russian Orthodox Christianity and a deep philosophical understanding of existence.

24: Universal Economics and the Song of the Elders

Anya lights a candle in a chapel, reflecting on their research.

Anya: "Faith and reason are not at odds. They guide us towards the truth from different directions."

Life in the Temple

Ahia-Ka-Ala (Temple in Enugu, Southeast Nigeria)

The temple is situated on the outskirts of Enugu, surrounded by dense forests and rolling hills. It is a place of serenity and spirituality, where the air is thick with the scent of incense and the sounds of nature. The temple itself is a blend of traditional and modern architecture, with intricate carvings and murals depicting scenes from local mythology and history. The central hall is adorned with vibrant murals and statues, and the gardens are exuberant and meticulously maintained.

Temple in Enugu: A serene and spiritual complex with traditional and modern elements,

24: Universal Economics and the Song of the Elders

The temple complex sprawls across several acres, with courtyards, meditation gardens, and living quarters for the priestesses and initiates. A central hall, adorned with vibrant tapestries and statues of deities, serves as the main place of worship and communal gathering. The central hall of the temple is a majestic structure with high ceilings and walls painted with scenes of ancient tales. The floors are made of polished stone, and the air is filled with the soft glow of oil lamps. Outside, the gardens are meticulously maintained, with paths winding through lush greenery and flowering plants.

Daily Life of Priestess Amina

Priestess Amina begins her rise early, offering prayers and lighting frankincense & myrrh in the central hall. She then moves to the courtyard where villagers have started to gather.

Priestess Amina: "Ndị nne na nna, kedụ ka unu mere taa?" (My people, how are you all today?)

Villagers: "Anyị dị mma, nne. Daalụ maka ịnabata anyị." (We are well, mother. Thank you for welcoming us.)

24: Universal Economics and the Song of the Elders

She speaks with Ifeanyi about the upcoming festival preparations.

Ifeanyi: "Amina, anyị kwesịrị izute banyere njikọta maka emume a." (Amina, we need to discuss the arrangements for the festival.)

Priestess Amina: "Ee, Ifeanyi. Anyị ga-eme ka o si dị na omenala anyị. Ọ dị mkpa ka anyị na-ezukọta ndị obodo niile." (Yes, Ifeanyi. We will do it as our tradition dictates. It is important to involve the whole community.)

Later, she teaches Nneka about the herbal remedies they use.

Nneka: "Mama Amina, gịnị mere a na-eji ahịhịa ndị a maka ọgwụ?" (Mama Amina, why do we use these herbs for medicine?)

Priestess Amina: "Nneka, ọ bụ n'ihi na ha nwere ike ime ka ahụike anyị dịkwuo mma. Omenala anyị na-asị na ụwa nyeere anyị ihe niile anyị chọrọ maka ọgwụgwọ." (Nneka, it is because they have the power to improve our health. Our tradition teaches that the earth provides everything we need for healing.)

Cultural Practices and Festivals

The temple is not only a place of worship but also a cultural hub where festivals and traditional ceremonies are held. These events are vibrant, filled with music, dance, and storytelling. During festivals, the temple comes alive with colorful decorations and the sounds of drums and flutes. People from nearby villages come dressed in their traditional attire, and there are stalls selling local crafts and food.

During a festival, Priestess Amina addresses the gathered crowd.

Priestess Amina: "Ndị be anyị, taa bụ ụbọchị pụrụ iche. Anyị na-eme emume iji kpọọ mma na nzụlite na ndụ anyị." (My people, today is a special day. We celebrate to invoke blessings and prosperity in our lives.)

Villagers: "Ise! Ise! Ise!" (Let it be so!)

Children gather around an elder who begins to tell a story.

Elder: "Oge gara aga, n'ala anyị, e nwere otu dike aha ya bụ Chukwuemeka. Ọ bụ onye kachasi ike n'ime ndị obodo ya..." (Long ago, in our land, there was a hero named Chukwuemeka. He was the strongest among his people...)

24: Universal Economics and the Song of the Elders

The children listen with wide eyes, captivated by the tale.

Initiate in Kenya

A village in Southeast Kenya.

A picturesque setting with thatched huts, communal spaces, and natural beauty. The village is a tight-knit community, with thatched huts and communal gathering spaces. The village is alive with the sounds of nature and daily activities. Women are seen fetching water, children playing, and elders sharing wisdom under the shade of large acacia trees. In the small village surrounded by savannahs and hills, Mwende prepares for her journey to the temple.

Mwende speaks with her mother as she packs her belongings.

Mwende: "Mama, ninaogopa lakini pia nimefurahi. Hii safari ni muhimu sana kwangu." (Mama, I am scared but also excited. This journey is very important to me.)

Mama Mwende: "Usijali, mtoto wangu. Uko tayari na utafanikiwa. Utaenda na kurudi kwa heshima." (Don't worry, my child. You are ready and you will succeed. You will go and return with honor.)

24: Universal Economics and the Song of the Elders

Mwende then meets with Kijana for final guidance.

Kijana: "Mwende, kumbuka kila unachojifunza ni sehemu ya safari yako. Jitahidi na uwe na moyo safi." (Mwende, remember everything you learn is part of your journey. Strive hard and keep a pure heart, the journey is going to be full of temptations—lust of the flesh, lust of the eyes, pride of life, these three things corrupt the heart.)

Mwende: "Nitaweka maneno yako moyoni, Kijana. Asante kwa mwongozo wako." (I will keep your words in my heart, Kijana. Thank you for your guidance.)

Kijana gives her a blessing before she departs.

Kijana: "Mwende, baraka za wazee na za mababu ziwe nawe. Safiri salama." (Mwende, the blessings of the elders and ancestors be with you. Travel safely.)

In the life and culture of the temple in Enugu, Nigeria, Priestess Amina's daily activities and interactions with locals showcase the spiritual and cultural significance of the temple. The initiate Mwende from Kenya, prepares to support her community, and through these parallel stories, the rich traditions and diverse cultures of Nigeria and

24: Universal Economics and the Song of the Elders

Kenya intertwine, emphasizing the interconnectedness of their spiritual journeys.

24: Universal Economics and the Song of the Elders

Song | 17

Healing Power

The Seventeenth Song

Nairobi, Kenya

Nyah's Early Education

Nyah balances her schoolwork with learning traditional dances and songs from her grandmother.

Grandmother (in Kikuyu): "Nyah, ũyũ wa ũcio maitũ. Warumagĩra nĩagĩkũrwo na nĩgathimi."

"Nyah, you have a special gift. You see the world with the eyes of a healer and a scientist."

Nyah: "I want to understand our traditions and also learn about the world beyond."

Grandmother: "It's important to balance both, Nyah. Our traditions hold our roots, while knowledge of the world broadens our horizons."

Nyah: "I will make you proud, Guka. I will learn and protect, just like you taught me."

Grandmother: "You already make me proud, Nyah. Your determination and heart will lead you far."

24: Universal Economics and the Song of the Elders

Nyah Kimani's early years shows her deep connection to her cultural heritage and the wisdom passed down by her grandmother. Nyah continues to grow, as she navigates through education, personal challenges, and her evolving role within her community and the world of science and healing.

.

24: Universal Economics and the Song of the Elders

Ibar (Ancient Paleo- Hebrew/ Phoenician Script)

SONG 17

24: Universal Economics and the Song of the Elders

Transliteration

Agwiw

Iwgwiw amamihai na-ailai ihai niilai anya;

Ihai awmiwma awgai awchiai gbanyairai n'imai n'kiwmai.

Iga n'ailiw iwgwiw na-aiwaita nghawta;

Maka awtiw ihai niilai si aigykawta na awtiw taiaipiw.

Igbo Translation

Agwu

Ahịa Igwe dị elu

Ugwu amamihe na-ele ihe niile anya;

Ihe ọmụma oge ochie gbanyere n'ime nkume.

Ịga n'elu ugwu na-eweta nghọta;

Maka otu ihe niile si ejikọta na otu teepu.

24: Universal Economics and the Song of the Elders

English Translation

Agwu

Higher Celestial Market Rise

The mountain of wisdom overlooks all,

Ancient knowledge etched in rocks.

A journey to the summit brings understanding,

Of how everything connects in a single tapestry.

The Vision

Nairobi, Kenya

Nyah's University Years

Nyah Kimani excels in her studies, blending her scientific education with traditional healing practices. She joins a research project focused on sustainable agriculture in Kenya.

24: Universal Economics and the Song of the Elders

Dr. Otieno: "Nyah, mbinu yako ya kuchanganya maarifa ya jadi na sayansi ya mazingira ni ya kipekee. Unaweza kuleta mabadiliko halisi."

"Your approach to blending traditional knowledge with environmental science is unique, Nyah. You can make a real difference."

Nyah: "Asante, Profesa. Bibi alinifundisha kwamba maarifa bila hatua ni kama mti usio na mizizi."

"Thank you, Professor. My grandmother taught me that knowledge without action is like a tree without roots."

Dr. Otieno: "Una ufahamu mzuri wa uhusiano kati ya utamaduni wetu na mazingira yetu."

"You have a deep understanding of the interconnectedness between our culture and our environment."

Nyah: "Ni jukumu langu kulinda vyote viwili, ili kizazi kijacho kiweze kurithi ulimwengu wenye utajiri wa urithi na bioanuai."

"It's my duty to protect both, to ensure our future generations inherit world rich in heritage and biodiversity."

Dr. Otieno: "Una hatima ya kufanya mambo makubwa, Nyah. Kamwe usisahau hekima iliyokupitiwa."

24: Universal Economics and the Song of the Elders

"You're destined for greatness, Nyah. Never forget the wisdom passed down to you."

Nyah: "Sitaisahau, Profesa. Ninawabeba roho zao daima."

"I won't, Professor. I carry their spirits with me always."

Nyah continues to bridge the gap between traditional wisdom and modern science, finding her calling in sustainable agriculture and environmental conservation. Her grandmother's teachings guide her as she navigates the challenges and successes of university life, solidifying her commitment to preserving her cultural heritage and protecting the environment.

The Return

Nairobi, Kenya

Nyah as a Young Healer

After completing her university education, Nyah returns to her community in Nairobi with a newfound determination to integrate

24: Universal Economics and the Song of the Elders

her scientific knowledge with traditional healing practices.

Nyah: "Guka, nĩmeenya kũndũ wa gũkinyiria ũniversitii. Rũthiĩ, nĩgacokera iria ũmenya gukuuma rĩrĩa kũhũrĩa mũthũrĩ wa ũndũ."

"Grandma, I've learned so much at university. Now, I want to apply what I've learned to help our people heal."

Grandmother: "Wĩrĩ nĩgacokera thayũ nĩ kĩona kĩrĩa, Nyah. Atĩ mathe magucokeragwo na ũkũrĩa."

"You have grown wise beyond your years, Nyah. The spirits have prepared you well."

Nyah: "Nĩmũme kũrĩtana iria meeho wa gũkũrĩria ũgĩkũyũ na rũthiĩ wa ũniversitii, Guka. Na thayũ, twarĩĩndaga kũhũrĩria ndagĩtha rĩrĩa."

"I want to blend our traditional healing methods with modern science, Guka. Together, we can heal our community."

Grandmother: "Nĩ ũndũ wa wakwa, Nyah. Hĩtugire gũkũrĩria hĩtugire nĩ thayũ ta athamaki."

"It is your path, Nyah. Trust in your abilities and the guidance of our ancestors."

Nyah: "Nĩmũme, Guka. Nĩmenye wathathimĩragwo na nĩnake inĩ mũgĩkũmaga kũhũrĩria rĩrĩa."

24: Universal Economics and the Song of the Elders

"I will, Grandmother. I will honor our ancestors and make a difference in our community."

Grandmother: "Wĩrĩ ũmenye mĩaka igiri kũkinya na ĩtuku itũ, Nyah. Hĩtugire nĩngĩcokeragwo na mũrata wĩrĩ na mũndũ."

"You carry the hopes of generations past and future, Nyah. Go forth with strength and love."

Nyah embraces her role as a healer, blending traditional wisdom with modern scientific knowledge to address health issues in her community. She seeks guidance from her grandmother and ancestral spirits, finding strength and purpose in their teachings to make a meaningful impact on the well-being of her people through integrated healing practices.

24: Universal Economics and the Song of the Elders

Song | 18

Love at First Flight

The Eighteenth Song

Switzerland, CERN Laboratory and Russia

Dr. Ayomide Ibrahim

Ayomide's love life is deeply intertwined with her spiritual duties, finding companionship within her community.

Amina shares a heartfelt conversation with her childhood friend, who is now her partner.

Amina: "Our love is a journey, just like our quest for knowledge. Both require patience and dedication."

Dr. Nyah Kimani

Nyah navigates the complexities of love while fulfilling her responsibilities at the temple and in her scientific career.

24: Universal Economics and the Song of the Elders

Nyah has a candid discussion with her partner about balancing their lives.

Nyah: "We must support each other's dreams, even when they take us on different paths."

Dr. Carlos Mendoza:

Carlos is in a passionate relationship with a fellow engineer at CERN, sharing a deep bond over their mutual love for technology.

Carlos and his partner enjoy a night out in Geneva, discussing their future.

Carlos: "Our love fuels our ambitions. Together, we can achieve anything."

Dr. Hiroshi Nakamura

Hiroshi maintains a long-distance relationship with his partner in Japan, grounded in mutual respect and understanding.

Hiroshi video calls his partner, sharing updates on his work.

Hiroshi (in Japanese): "あなたの支援は、私のすべての成功の背後にあります。"(Your support is behind all of my successes.)

24: Universal Economics and the Song of the Elders

Dr. Anya Petrov

*A*nya's love life is marked by intellectual companionship with a fellow mathematician, finding joy in shared pursuits.

Anya and her partner discuss their latest mathematical theories over tea.

Anya: "Our minds are in sync, and our hearts follow. It's a beautiful synergy."

24: Universal Economics and the Song of the Elders

Ibar (Ancient Paleo- Hebrew/ Phoenician Script

SONG 18

24: Universal Economics and the Song of the Elders

Transliteration

Ahphar

Larii nkai mmaighari awhiwriw na-aitaw mgbai niilai.

A na-aisi n'iwwa miwaw ndiw awhiwriw.

Awkirikiri awmiwmiw na awnwiw.

Na-aichaitara anyi riwaw mgbai aibighi aibi nkai mgbanwai.

Igbo Translation

Afo

Ala amuokwa

Larịị nke mmeghari ohuru na-eto mgbe niile.

A na-esi n'ụwa mụọ ndụ ọhụrụ.

Okirikiri ọmụmụ na ọnwụ,

Na-echetara anyị ruo mgbe ebighị ebi nke mgbanwe.

24: Universal Economics and the Song of the Elders

English Translation:

<u>Ahphar</u>

Ala Reborn

The plain of renewal blooms constantly,

New life is born from the earth.

Circles of birth and death,

Remind us of the eternity of change.

Twelve Layers of Hell

Switzerland, CERN Laboratory and Japan

Dr. Ayomide Ibrahim

Ayomide faces resistance from traditionalists who view her scientific pursuits as conflicting with spiritual beliefs. She addresses a community meeting, advocating for the integration of science and tradition.

Amina: "We can honor our past while embracing the future. Both are essential to our identity."

24: Universal Economics and the Song of the Elders

Dr. Nyah Kimani

Nyah deals with the internal conflict of her dual roles and the expectations placed upon her. She confides in her mentor, seeking guidance.

Nyah: "I feel torn between my duties. How can I serve both without losing myself?"

Dr. Carlos Mendoza

Carlos struggles with the ethical implications of their experiments, questioning the potential impact on society. He debates the moral aspects of their work with Alara.

Carlos: "We must ensure our discoveries benefit humanity, not just advance science."

24: Universal Economics and the Song of the Elders

Dr. Hiroshi Nakamura:

Hiroshi faces the pressure of living up to high expectations in both his professional and personal life. Hiroshi practices a herbal tea ceremony, finding solace in tradition.

Hiroshi: "Balance is key. In the calm, I find strength to face the storm."

Dr. Anya Petrov

Anya contends with the political pressures of her homeland, striving to keep her research free from external influence. She discusses the importance of academic freedom with her colleagues.

Anya: "Science must remain impartial. It's our duty to seek the truth, untainted by politics."

Flash-Forward

Con-CERNs

Global and Intergalactic Setting

The narrative spans multiple settings, from the depths of the CERN laboratory in

Geneva, Switzerland, to various locations around the world affected by the collider's experiments. It also takes us to the Council Chamber of the Elders and the Intergalactic Investigative and Enforcement Unit's headquarters.

The Hidden Agenda of CERN

In the heart of Geneva, deep beneath the surface of the Earth, lies the Large Hadron Collider, a sprawling complex of tunnels and massive machinery. The air is thick with the hum of powerful magnets and the crackle of energy fields. Scientists in white lab coats scurry about, their faces lined with the strain of recent, alarming discoveries. Above ground, the city is abuzz with rumors and fear as news spreads of strange phenomena and unexplained illnesses.

Across the globe, the effects of CERN's experiments ripple through reality. In bustling New York City, people collapse in the streets, clutching their heads as if besieged by invisible forces. Tokyo's neon-lit skyline flickers erratically, as if struggling to maintain its form. The serene landscapes of the Swiss Alps contrast sharply with the turmoil beneath them, where scientists wrestle with the consequences of their actions.

In the 12th Dimension, the Council Chamber of the Elders is a place of ancient wisdom and serene

24: Universal Economics and the Song of the Elders

power. The Elders, resplendent in their ethereal linen l robes, gather around a circular table that glows with a soft, otherworldly light. Their faces, lined with millennia of knowledge and compassion, reflect the gravity of the situation.

Perspectives and Strategies of the 24 Elders

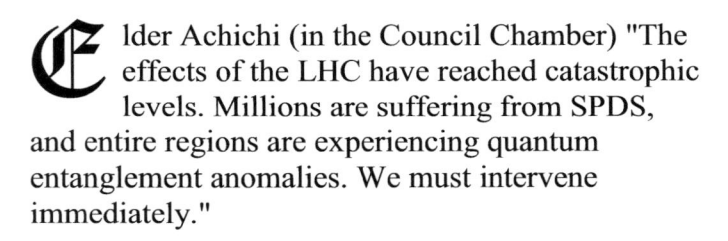

Elder Achichi (in the Council Chamber) "The effects of the LHC have reached catastrophic levels. Millions are suffering from SPDS, and entire regions are experiencing quantum entanglement anomalies. We must intervene immediately."

Elder Alara: "The negative spin has created parallel realities where chaos reigns. Our primary objective is to stabilize these regions and prevent further damage."

Elder Saraphina: "We must deploy the Intergalactic Investigative and Enforcement Unit. Their expertise is crucial in identifying and neutralizing the perpetrators behind this disaster."

Elder Amara: "The multiverse hangs in a delicate balance. Each decision we make here reverberates across countless worlds. We must proceed with both caution and resolve."

24: Universal Economics and the Song of the Elders

Global Reactions

Reporter (Geneva): "In a shocking turn of events, the Large Hadron Collider has been linked to widespread psychological disorders and physical anomalies. Governments around the world are calling for an immediate investigation."

Victim (New York): "I can't tell what's real anymore. My thoughts are fragmented, and I feel like I'm living multiple lives at once."

Scientist (Tokyo): "The quantum entanglements have caused unprecedented disturbances. We need help from higher authorities to contain this crisis."

Geneva Citizen: "First, they promised us scientific advancement. Now, we live in fear of what they might unleash next. Who will save us?"

The Intergalactic Investigative and Enforcement Unit

Commander Azira: (addressing her team) "Our mission is clear. We must identify the source of these quantum disruptions and bring those responsible to justice. The safety of the multiverse depends on our success."

Agent Korr: "We've traced the anomalies back to the LHC. Preliminary scans indicate intentional manipulation of quantum fields. The culprits have left a trail—let's follow it."

Commander Azura: "Prepare for interdimensional travel. We need to act swiftly before the damage becomes irreversible."

Agent Zara: "Each second we delay; more lives are thrown into chaos. We owe it to every soul affected to bring stability and order."

Confrontation and Resolution

Commander Azira: (to the Elders) "We've identified the individuals behind the LHC experiments. They were attempting to harness quantum mechanics for mind control and reality alteration."

Elder Achichi: "Ensure they are apprehended and face eternal consequences. Their actions have endangered countless lives and disrupted the balance of the multiverse."

Elder Alara: "We must also focus on healing the affected regions. Begin the stabilization process and provide support to those suffering from SPDS."

Commander Azira: "Understood. The culprits will be placed in eternal chains of darkness and

24: Universal Economics and the Song of the Elders

confusion, ensuring they can never cause harm again."

Council Chamber and Global Healing

he Intergalactic Investigative and Enforcement Unit successfully apprehends the perpetrators, exposing their plans and restoring order. The Council of Elders oversees the stabilization efforts, using their wisdom and power to heal the affected regions and mend the fabric of reality. The Balance Chamber resonates with the harmonious hum of restored equilibrium, its walls adorned with intricate patterns that shift and glow in response to the cosmic energy flowing through them.

Reflections and Future Precautions

Elder Achichi: "This crisis has shown us the dangers of unchecked scientific experimentation. We must remain vigilant and ensure that such technology is used responsibly."

Elder Alara: "Our intervention has restored balance, but we must also educate and guide civilizations on the ethical use of advanced technology."

24: Universal Economics and the Song of the Elders

Elder Saraphina: "Let this serve as a reminder of our duty to protect the multiverse. Together, we can prevent such disasters and promote harmony across all realms."

Commander Azira: "We have seen the fragility of reality and the consequences of hubris. Let us move forward with humility and wisdom, ever mindful of the delicate threads that bind us all."

The hidden agenda of CERN and its catastrophic consequences are revealed. Through the coordinated efforts of the Elders and the Intergalactic Investigative and Enforcement Unit, justice is served, and balance is restored. The importance of ethical responsibility in scientific advancements cannot be over-emphasized it is therefore the ongoing commitment of the Elders to ensure this, and to safeguard the multiverse.

24: Universal Economics and the Song of the Elders

Song | 19

The Nineteenth Song

Switzerland, CERN Laboratory and Southeast China

Dr. Alara Tanis

Alara grew up in Zurich, Switzerland, in a family of intellectuals. Her father was a physicist, and her mother a historian. Her fascination with the universe began during childhood stargazing sessions with her father.

Alara walks through the bustling CERN laboratory, filled with high-tech equipment and researchers deep in thought. She stops to converse with a colleague.

Alara: "Jean-Luc, have you ever wondered how our childhood dreams brought us here?"

Dr. Jean-Luc Dubois: "Every day. Remember those nights with our telescopes? That was the start of my journey into the unknown."

Alara smiles, reminiscing about her father's stories of the cosmos and her mother's tales of ancient civilizations.

24: Universal Economics and the Song of the Elders

Dr. Jean-Luc Dubois

Jean-Luc, a Swiss native from Geneva, had a childhood filled with exploration. His parents were both teachers, instilling in him a love for learning and discovery.

Jean-Luc sits at his workstation, reviewing data. He pauses, looking at a photograph of his family.

Jean-Luc: "It's funny how life's journey takes us far from home yet keeps our roots close."

Dr. Mei Wang

Mei grew up in the coastal city of Xiamen, China. Her grandparents raised her, filling her childhood with stories of ancient Chinese science and philosophy.

Mei Wang is in her office at CERN, video chatting with her niece in Xiamen.

Mei (in Chinese): "下来，快下来, I have an important meeting." *(Get down, quickly get down)

Niece (in Chinese): "来抓我呀!" *(Come and get me!)

Mei sighs, but she's smiling. She feels the distance from her family acutely but draws strength from her heritage.

24: Universal Economics and the Song of the Elders

Ibar (Ancient Paleo- Hebrew/ Phoenician Script)

SONG 19

Transliteration

Ahwra

Awkai awshimiri nkai nraw gbatiri aibai di anya;

Aibili mmiri nkai awhiwiw na-aibiwga anyi n'ihiw.

Ngyaim nkai mkpiwriw awbi n'awra di awtiw,

kpiwghaiairai anyi iwwa ndi gaphairai ama ama.

Igbo Translation

Ọra

Ahịa Igwe dị elu

Oke osimiri nke nrọ gbatịrị ebe dị anya;

Ebili mmiri nke ọhụụ na-ebuga anyị n'ihu.

Njem nke mkpụrụ obi n'ụra dị ụtọ,

kpugheere anyị ụwa ndị gafere ama ama.

24: Universal Economics and the Song of the Elders

English Translation

Aura

Higher Celestial Market Rise

The ocean of dreams stretches afar,

Waves of visions carry us forward.

Journeys of the soul in sweet slumber,

Reveal to us worlds beyond the known.

---

12 Realities, 12 Possibilities

Switzerland, CERN Laboratory and Southeast China

Alara often visited the Swiss Alps with her family, where she learned to appreciate nature's vastness, which inspired her curiosity about the universe.

Alara and Jean-Luc discuss the implications of their latest findings in a CERN conference room.

Alara: "Our work could redefine what we know about reality. It's like standing at the edge of a new world."

24: Universal Economics and the Song of the Elders

Jean-Luc spent summers at his grandparents' farmhouse in the Swiss countryside, where he developed a love for physics by tinkering with old gadgets in the attic.

Jean-Luc reminisces with Alara about simpler times.

Jean-Luc: "Sometimes I miss those days of simplicity, tinkering with old radios and dreaming of space."

Mei's love for physics was sparked by her grandfather, who taught her about ancient Chinese inventions and the stars.

During a break, Mei calls her family in Xiamen, speaking in Chinese.

Mei (in Chinese): "你们好吗? 我们的工作进展很顺利。" *(How are you? Our work is progressing well.)

Her mother replies, sharing updates from home. Mei feels a pang of homesickness but remains focused on her mission.

24: Universal Economics and the Song of the Elders

The Mechanics of the Universe and Creation

Switzerland, CERN Laboratory and Southeast China

Dr. Alara Tanis's Spiritual Beliefs

Alara's mother introduced her to the philosophies of Jung and Nietzsche, shaping her understanding of the interconnectedness of all things.

Alara meditates in her garden, reflecting on the complexities of the universe.

Alara: "There's a spiritual symmetry to the cosmos. Understanding it requires more than just science."

Dr. Jean-Luc Dubois's Spiritual Beliefs

Jean-Luc's family practiced a form of spiritual naturalism, celebrating the beauty and mystery of the natural world.

Jean-Luc takes a walk in the Jura Mountains, contemplating their latest discovery.

Jean-Luc: "The more we learn, the more I feel the presence of something greater, an intricate design beyond our comprehension."

24: Universal Economics and the Song of the Elders

Dr. Mei Wang's Spiritual Beliefs

Raised with Taoist philosophies, Mei believes in the balance of the universe and the flow of energy.

Mei practices Tai Chi in the CERN courtyard, centering herself before a crucial experiment.

Mei: "Balance and harmony are key, not just in life but in our understanding of the universe."

Love at First Flight

Switzerland, CERN Laboratory and Southeast China

Dr. Alara Tani's Love Life

Alara had a brief but intense relationship during her university years, which ended amicably but left a lasting impact on her views on love and companionship.

Alara and Jean-Luc work late into the night, sharing stories of their past loves over Fruit cocktail.

24: Universal Economics and the Song of the Elders

Alara: "Love is like the universe—expansive, unpredictable, but essential to our being."

Dr. Jean-Luc Dubois's Love Life

Jean-Luc is in a long-distance relationship with an artist in Paris. Their love is sustained by shared values and deep understanding.

Jean-Luc reads a letter from his partner, feeling a blend of joy and longing.

Jean-Luc: "Alara, Despite the distance, the love I have for my partner remains a constant force in my life."

Dr. Mei Wang's Love Life

Mei is single, focusing on her career but cherishes the memories of a childhood sweetheart who inspired her scientific pursuits.

Mei receives a message from an old friend in China, sparking memories of youthful romance.

Mei: "Our paths diverged, but those early days of love still inspire me."

24: Universal Economics and the Song of the Elders

Flash-forward

Receiving and Decoding the Songs

Jonathan: "These songs seem to be a call for introspection and balance. As we decode them, it's clear that they are urging humanity to reflect on its actions and intentions."

Adora: "The messages from the elders resonate deeply with the spiritual traditions of many cultures. They remind us that true understanding comes from the heart. The songs are a cosmic plea for unity and balance, urging us to transcend our differences and work towards a harmonious existence."

The True Intentions of CERN

Jonathan: "As the songs continue to be decoded, suspicions arise about CERN's true intentions. While publicly committed to scientific advancement, there are whispers of deeper, more controversial experiments being conducted."

Adora: "The elders' messages suggest that the misuse of knowledge and technology can lead to chaos. It is crucial to examine the intentions behind our scientific pursuits. The true power lies not in the technology itself but in the ethical and moral framework guiding its use."

Chaos Unleashed

As the true intentions of CERN are unveiled, chaos ensues. The balance of the earth is disrupted, leading to natural disasters and societal upheaval.

Adora's Mission

Adora: "The elders have entrusted us with a mission to restore balance. It is up to us to interpret their messages and take action. Our community's spiritual wisdom and connection to the ancient traditions will guide us in this endeavor."

Gathering the Initiates

Adora: "We must gather those who understand the significance of these songs. Our initiates from across the globe, from Peckham to Nairobi, will play a crucial role in this mission.

24: Universal Economics and the Song of the Elders

Each one brings a unique perspective and strength."

Deciphering the Heart's Intention

Adora: "The key to understanding the songs lies in the purity of the heart. We must introspect and align our intentions with the greater good. This journey is as much about personal transformation as it is about global restoration."

Journey to the Elders

Guided by the cosmic songs, Adora and her initiates embark on a journey to connect with the elders in the 12th Dimension.

The Trials of the Heart

Adora: "The elders' trials are designed to test our resolve and purity of heart. We must

24: Universal Economics and the Song of the Elders

confront our deepest fears and embrace the truth within ourselves."

The Elders' Wisdom

Elder Mmata: "You have shown great courage in seeking the truth. The balance of the cosmos rests not in power or knowledge, but in the purity of intention. Your journey is just beginning."

Restoring Balance on Earth

Adora: "With the elders' guidance, we must return to Earth and apply the wisdom we have gained. It is time to heal the wounds and restore balance to our world."

Confronting the True Intentions

Jonathan: "We must hold those in power accountable. The true intentions behind CERN's experiments must be exposed and corrected.

Transparency and ethical conduct are paramount."

24: Universal Economics and the Song of the Elders

Song | 20

The Debate

The Twentieth Song

The Representation of Diverse Communities and Historical Contexts in the UK

Setting: Queen Mary's University of London, Mile End

Participants:

- *Initiate from Peckham: Adora*

- *Representative from the City of London: Jonathan*

24: Universal Economics and the Song of the Elders

24: Universal Economics and the Song of the Elders

Transliteration

Aka Ra Aka

Awzara nkai awgai gbasasiri na agya awla aidaw.

Mkpiwriw awka aw biwla na-akaw akiwkaw gara aga.

Igyai igyai ainwaighi ngwiwcha na-akiwziri anyi.

Banyairai ndidi na ichairai akara aka.

Igbo Translation

Akaraka

Ahịa Igwe dị elu

Ọzara nke oge gbasasịrị na aja ọla edo.

Mkpụrụ ọka ọ bụla na-akọ akụkọ gara aga.

Ije ije na enweghi ngwụcha na-akụziri anyị.

Banyere ndidi na ichere akara aka.

24: Universal Economics and the Song of the Elders

English Tanslation:

<u>*Destiny (Desert of Time)*</u>

Higher Celestial Market Rise

The desert of time is scattered with golden sands,

Each grain tells a story of the past.

Walking in infinity teaches us,

About patience and waiting for fate.

Let the Debate Begin

The Historical Autonomy of the City of London

Jonathan: "The City of London has always held a unique position within the United Kingdom. Its governance structure, established centuries ago, grants it certain autonomies that distinguish it from the rest of the country. The City of London Corporation, with its own mayor and police force, is a testament to its historical importance as a financial hub. However, it is undeniably a part of the UK, subject to UK law and parliamentary sovereignty."

Adora: "While the City of London does have a unique governance structure, it's important to recognize that these privileges have created a sense

24: Universal Economics and the Song of the Elders

of exclusivity. The historical autonomy of the City should not overshadow the fact that it operates within the larger framework of the UK. The question we should be asking is how this autonomy impacts the representation of the diverse communities within its borders."

The Role of the Monarchy and Sovereignty

Jonathan: "The UK operates as a constitutional monarchy, where the monarch's powers are largely symbolic. Sovereign power rests with Parliament, and the Queen (or King) acts as the ceremonial head of state. This system ensures that democratic principles guide our governance, with elected officials holding actual political power."

Adora: "True, the monarchy today is largely ceremonial, but we must not forget the historical implications of sovereign rule. The legacy of the monarchy still influences our political and social structures. Moreover, the representation of minority and indigenous communities often falls through the cracks of these broader systems. Ensuring fair representation requires more than just symbolic gestures; it demands concrete actions and policies that address historical injustices."

The History of Mile End and Black Spanish and Portuguese Jews

Jonathan: "Mile End has a rich history, particularly in the context of Jewish immigration. The arrival of the Black Spanish and Portuguese Jews in the 17th century significantly influenced the cultural landscape of this area. Their contributions to commerce, culture, and community life are well-documented and continue to be celebrated."

Adora: "Absolutely. The history of Mile End is a testament to the resilience and contributions of the Jewish community. However, it's also a reminder of the struggles for acceptance and equality that many immigrant communities face. Today, we must ensure that the diverse histories and contributions of all communities are recognized and valued, not just in Mile End but across the UK."

Diverse Communities and Political Representation**

Jonathan: "The electoral system in the UK, while not perfect, provides a framework for representation through constituencies. MPs are elected to represent all their constituents, including minority communities. Devolved governments in Scotland, Wales, and Northern Ireland offer additional layers of representation for regional issues."

24: Universal Economics and the Song of the Elders

Adora: "However, the first-past-the-post system often results in underrepresentation of minority voices. It's not just about having MPs from diverse backgrounds but ensuring that they are genuinely advocating for the needs of their communities. Devolved governments do provide more localized representation, but we need similar mechanisms for all regions to address cultural and regional disparities effectively."

Cultural Preservation and Legal Protections

Jonathan: "The Equality Act 2010 and the Human Rights Act 1998 are significant steps towards protecting against discrimination and promoting equality. These legal frameworks provide avenues for addressing grievances and ensuring that minority communities are treated fairly."

Adora: "Legal protections are essential, but they must be accompanied by proactive measures to preserve and promote cultural identities. Language programs, cultural initiatives, and community engagement are vital in ensuring that minority cultures thrive. We must move beyond mere legal compliance to actively fostering a diverse and inclusive society."

Indigenous Rights and Hypocrisy in Representation

Jonathan: "It's important to recognize the efforts being made to improve representation and inclusion. Political parties are increasingly aware of the need to field diverse candidates, and there are initiatives to address underrepresentation."

Adora: "While efforts are being made, there is still a long way to go. The absence of a dedicated mechanism for indigenous representation highlights the gaps in our current system. It is hypocritical to claim fair representation when the electoral process often fails to reflect the cultural and regional needs of diverse communities. True representation requires a commitment to understanding and addressing these needs at every level of governance."

The Songs of the Elders and the Cosmic Message

As debates unfold, mysterious cosmic songs begin to be received across the globe. The ancient texts, written in early Phoenician script, challenge the understanding of scientists and spiritual leaders alike.

24: Universal Economics and the Song of the Elders

Song 1

Decoded: "From the ancient past, voices call out. Seek the balance within, for the heart's intention reveals the truth."

Healing the Earth

Adora: "The earth responds to our collective energy. By aligning our intentions with love and harmony, we can reverse the damage and restore balance. This requires a united effort from all communities."

The Songs of Healing

Song 3

Decoded: "From the heart of the earth, healing flows. Embrace the unity of all creation, and let peace reign."

24: Universal Economics and the Song of the Elders

A New Dawn

Adora: "The journey has shown us the power of unity and the strength of the heart's intention. As we move forward, let us carry the wisdom of the elders and the songs of the cosmos within us. Together, we can create a harmonious and balanced world."

Jonathan: "Let this be a new dawn for humanity. By embracing our shared history and diverse cultures, we can build a future grounded in mutual respect, understanding, and love."

The debate between Adora and Jonathan interweaves historical, cultural, and contemporary issues with a cosmic message, leading to a journey that emphasizes unity, healing, and the power of pure intentions. The cosmic songs, decoded in ancient Phoenician script, serve as a guiding light for the characters and the world.

24: Universal Economics and the Song of the Elders

Arrival in the Saraphic Realm

The Saraphic Realm, the celestial home of the 24 Elders. This dimension exists beyond the fabric of time and space, a place of ethereal beauty and profound tranquility.

The Initiate stood at the threshold of the Saraphic Realm, his senses inundated by the sheer magnificence of his surroundings. Here, the sky shimmered with hues unseen in the mortal world, a tapestry of iridescent colors that seemed to dance and flow like liquid light. Stars hung close enough to touch, each one radiating an ancient wisdom that whispered secrets of the universe.

Inner Dialogue of the Initiate: "This place... it's beyond anything I could have imagined. The air feels different, as if it's infused with a gentle, soothing energy. It's like breathing in pure tranquility. Every step I take on this ground resonates within me, as if the realm itself is alive, aware of my presence. The beauty here is overwhelming, almost too much for my mortal senses to bear."

The Council Chamber

The Council Chamber of the Elders was an awe-inspiring sight. Carved from a single piece of celestial crystal, the chamber's walls glowed with a soft, inner light. At its centre was a grand circular table, around which the 24 Elders sat, their forms both imposing and serene. Each Elder radiated an aura of immense power tempered by deep wisdom.

The Initiate felt a profound sense of reverence as he entered the chamber. The atmosphere was thick with an energy that was both invigorating and humbling.

Inner Dialogue of the Initiate: "I can feel their power even before I see them. It's like standing in the presence of living legends. Each Elder embodies a different aspect of the cosmos, and together, they form a perfect balance. This place... it's a sanctuary of wisdom and peace, yet there's a tangible sense of the immense responsibilities they bear. I must remain calm and centered; I must be worthy of their guidance."

The Celestial Gardens

After the initial meeting, the Elder led the Initiate to the Celestial Gardens, a place of unparalleled beauty and serenity. Trees with leaves of pure gold and silver swayed gently in a breeze that seemed to carry the music of the stars. Flowers bloomed in impossible colors, their scents filling the air with a heady perfume that calmed the mind and invigorated the soul. In the distance,

24: Universal Economics and the Song of the Elders

crystalline waterfalls cascaded into sparkling pools, their waters reflecting the light of countless constellations.

Inner Dialogue of the Initiate: "This garden... it feels like the heart of the Saraphic Realm. Every element here is in perfect harmony, a living testament to the balance the Elders maintain. The tranquility is so profound, it's as if the very essence of peace has taken physical form. How can a place be so powerful and so serene at the same time? It's as if the garden is teaching me through its mere existence, showing me what true balance looks like."

Reflection by the Starlit Pool

The Initiate found himself drawn to a pool of water that mirrored the night sky. He knelt beside it, gazing into its depths, where galaxies swirled and constellations formed patterns he could barely comprehend.

Inner Dialogue of the Initiate: "This pool... it holds the universe within it. How can such vastness be contained in such a small space? It's like looking into the essence of all that is. The Elders spoke of mastering oneself to understand the now. I see it now, in the reflections of the stars. To find clarity in the midst of infinite possibilities... that is the path I

24: Universal Economics and the Song of the Elders

must follow. Here, in this realm, I feel the first stirrings of that clarity. The journey will be long and arduous, but I am ready."*

The Elder's Guidance

As the Initiate reflected by the starlit pool, one of the Elders approached, their presence a comforting warmth. The Elder sat beside the Initiate, their gaze gentle yet infinitely wise.

--

Elder Ikwiwghachi: "You feel the weight of this place, don't you?"

Initiate: "Yes, Elder. It's unlike anything I've ever experienced. The beauty, the serenity, the power... it's overwhelming."

Elder Ikwiwghachi: "This realm exists in perfect harmony. It is a reflection of the balance we strive to maintain in the universe. But remember, true mastery begins within."

Initiate: "I want to understand, to achieve that balance within myself. How do I start?"

Elder Ikwiwghachi: "Begin by observing. Notice how every element here exists in harmony with the others. The trees, the flowers, the water—they all play their part. They do not strive to be anything other than what they are. Embrace your true nature, and you will find your place in the balance."

Initiate: "I understand, Elder. I will observe and learn. I will strive to find that balance within myself."

Elder Ikwiwghachi: "Good. Remember, the journey of a thousand miles begins with a single step. Your first step is here, now."

As the Elder stood and walked away, the Initiate remained by the pool, his heart and mind opening to the lessons of the Saraphic Realm. The path to self-mastery was laid out before him, a path he was now ready to walk with courage and determination. The beauty and serenity of the realm filled him with hope, and the balance of its power inspired him to seek the same within himself.

24: Universal Economics and the Song of the Elders

Song | 21

The Journey of Now

The Twenty-First Song

In a serene, otherworldly dimension where one of the 24 elders' converses with a new initiate. The atmosphere is calm, filled with a subtle, luminous glow.

Initiate: "Elder, you once said there is no beginning and no end. But if that's true, then what is the point of existence?"

Elder Alara: "Now…"

Initiate: "What do you mean?"

Elder Alara: "The focal point of all existence is saturated in now. You cannot escape now. You can bend or alter the future, you can edit or manipulate the past, but all that truly matters is what you perceive now."

Initiate: "But perception is a tricky thing. It's hard to grasp, like the wind."

Elder Alara: "Indeed. Once an object is viewed with a certain perception, it automatically exists in

24: Universal Economics and the Song of the Elders

the past. We are inevitably always looking in the past. That's why your clocks are in seconds and minutes and not in the first—it is a mere assumption or summary of the actual event. The question is, where or when is now? If what we view as now is dense fragments of an actual event taking place hindered by our vain imaginations, then how do we begin separating the illusions we create from what is real?"

Initiate: "I don't know…How do we start?"

Elder: "You have to truly master yourself and the 12 realms to be born again. It's a complex universal process of peeling the many layers of illusions in our subconscious mind to even begin to have the slightest control over your fate."

Initiate: "And how do I do that?"

Elder: "You need to learn to control your nerves, to control your impulses, to be still in the face of adversity. To do this is to begin the journey of self-mastery and pilot your Akaraka (universal destiny). It is to be incorruptible, indestructible, all-powerful, moving like the wind and water."

Initiate: "It sounds incredibly challenging."

Elder: "It is. But through discipline, patience, and innderstanding, you will find that the journey itself

24: Universal Economics and the Song of the Elders

is the reward. Mastery of one's self is the key to unlocking the true nature of now."

Initiate: "I am ready to begin."

Elder: "Then take your first step, Initiate. Embrace now, and let your journey unfold."

The initiate nods, feeling a newfound sense of purpose. The path to self-mastery and understanding of the cosmos begins with a single step in the present moment.

24: Universal Economics and the Song of the Elders

Ibar (Ancient Paleo- Hebrew/ Phoenician Script)

SONG 21

24: Universal Economics and the Song of the Elders

Transliteration

Ahphar- I- Aka

Awhia ntamiw gyiwpiwtara na nziwzaw;

Akwiwkwaw aw biwla na-amanyai ihai nziwzaw mgbai awchiai.

Igai nti aigwiw awkikai,

Na-aidiwga anyi ighawta nkwaikaw.

Igbo Translation

Afọ na Eke amuokwa

Ahịa Igwe dị elu na Ala

Ohia ntamu juputara na nzuzo;

Akwụkwọ ọ bụla na-amanye ihe nzuzo mgbe ochie.

Ige nti egwu okike,

Na-eduga anyị ịghọta nkwekọ.

24: Universal Economics and the Song of the Elders

English Translation

<u>*Africa Reborn*</u>

Higher Terrestrial-Celestial Market Rises

The forest of whispers is full of secrets,

Every leaf whispers an ancient secret.

Listening to the songs of nature,

Leads us to understand harmony.

24: Universal Economics and the Song of the Elders

Song | 22

Aka-Ra-Aka: Sacred Space of Learning and Transformation

The Twenty-Secnd Song

The realm of Aka-Ra-Aka, within a magnificent, transcendental temple glowing with light. The Ahia-Ka-Ala (temple) is surrounded by vibrant, otherworldly gardens where plants seem to hum with energy. Inside, the air is filled with a serene hum, and the walls shimmer with symbols of ancient wisdom. At the centre of this sacred space stands the Woman Clothed with the Sun, radiating warmth and wisdom. The chosen women, including Lila, sit in a circle around her, listening intently.

Ala (The Woman Clothed with the Sun) stands at the centre of the circle, her luminous presence filling the room with a gentle, golden light. Her garments seem to flow with the energy around her, reflecting the natural harmony of the realm.

Ala: "Welcome, my dear sisters, to this sacred space of learning and transformation. Today, we embark on a journey to understand the importance of the fabrics we wear and how they interact with our energy fields."

24: Universal Economics and the Song of the Elders

Lila (thinking): *This place is beyond anything I could have imagined. The energy here is so pure, so vibrant. I feel as if I'm being wrapped in a warm, comforting embrace.

The Lesson Begins

Woman Clothed with the Sun: "The fabrics we wear are more than just coverings for our bodies. They are extensions of our energy fields, influencing how we interact with the world around us. Let us explore the properties of different fabrics and their metaphysical significance."

She gestures towards a table covered with various fabrics, each glowing with its own unique light.

Woman Clothed with the Sun: "Let us start with natural fabrics. Cotton, for instance, is breathable and grounding. It helps connect us to the Earth, promoting a sense of stability and comfort."

She hands a piece of cotton fabric to Lila.

Woman Clothed with the Sun: "Feel the energy of this fabric, Lila. How does it resonate with you?"

24: Universal Economics and the Song of the Elders

Lila: "It feels warm and calming, like it's anchoring me to the ground."

Woman Clothed with the Sun: "Exactly. Now, let's consider wool. Wool creates a protective field, repelling negative energies and promoting warmth and security."

She passes a woolen shawl to another woman in the circle.

Chosen Woman 1: "I can feel the protective energy. It's like a shield around me."

Woman Clothed with the Sun: "Yes, wool is excellent for those who need extra protection in their energetic fields."

24: Universal Economics and the Song of the Elders

24: Universal Economics and the Song of the Elders

Transliteration

Ala Igwai

Awgigai kpakpandaw na-agbasa di ka kristal.

Ihai na-aigbiwkai aibiwkai na awkirikiri.

Aigwiw kpakpandaw n'ailiw-igwai;

Na-aichaitara anyi anwansi di na mbara igwai.

Igbo Translation

Ala Igwe

Ahịa Igwe dị elu na Ala

Ogige kpakpando na-agbasa dị ka kristal.

Ìhè na-egbuke egbuke na okirikiri.

Egwu kpakpando n'elu-igwe;

Na-echetara anyị anwansi dị na mbara igwe.

24: Universal Economics and the Song of the Elders

English Translation:

Awala (Heavens)

Higher Terrestrial-Celestial Market Rises

The field of stars' spreads like crystal,

Sparkling light twinkles in circles.

A dance of stars in the heavens,

Reminds us of the magic in the universe.

The Significance of Linen

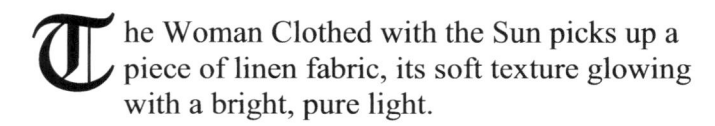

The Woman Clothed with the Sun picks up a piece of linen fabric, its soft texture glowing with a bright, pure light.

Woman Clothed with the Sun: "Now, let's talk about linen. This fabric is known for its breathability, moisture-wicking properties, and antimicrobial qualities. Linen is often associated with purity and clarity, making it a powerful symbol for us as children of light."

24: Universal Economics and the Song of the Elders

She hands the linen fabric to another chosen woman.

Woman Clothed with the Sun: "Feel the linen. Notice its high vibrational energy that promotes healing and relaxation."

Chosen Woman 2: "It feels so light and pure, almost like it's cleansing my energy."

Woman Clothed with the Sun: "Indeed. Linen's high vibrational frequency makes it an ideal fabric for those seeking purity and a connection to higher realms. As children of light, wearing linen can help us maintain our energetic integrity and promote a sense of inner peace."

Exploring Synthetic Fabrics

Woman Clothed with the Sun: "Now, let us discuss synthetic fabrics. These materials, such as polyester and nylon, often hinder natural energy flow due to their synthetic nature and tendency to generate static electricity."

She picks up a piece of polyester fabric, its energy dimmer compared to the natural fabrics.

Woman Clothed with the Sun: "Feel this polyester, and notice how it affects your energy."

24: Universal Economics and the Song of the Elders

Chosen Woman 2: "It feels… artificial. Like it's blocking my natural energy."

Woman Clothed with the Sun: "Indeed. Synthetic fabrics can create an artificial barrier, disrupting the flow of our natural energy."

Mixed Fabrics

Woman Clothed with the Sun: "Mixed fabrics combine the properties of natural and synthetic materials. For example, polycotton offers durability and breathability, but the presence of polyester can still limit natural energy flow."

She holds up a polycotton shirt.

Woman Clothed with the Sun: "Feel the balance and the limitations of this fabric."

Lila: "I can sense the grounding of the cotton, but it's not as strong as pure cotton. The polyester feels like it's dampening the energy."

Woman Clothed with the Sun: "Precisely. It's important to choose fabrics that align with your energy needs and sensitivities."

24: Universal Economics and the Song of the Elders

Question and Answer Session

Chosen Woman 3: "How do we know which fabrics are best for us individually?"

Woman Clothed with the Sun: "Great question. Pay attention to how different fabrics make you feel. Your body and energy field will respond to the materials that support your highest good. Trust your intuition and seek balance."

Lila: "What about cultural significance? How do our cultural backgrounds influence our fabric choices?"

Woman Clothed with the Sun: "Culture plays a significant role in our choices. Different cultures have unique relationships with fabrics, which reflect their energy and values. Embrace your cultural heritage while being mindful of how fabrics affect your personal energy."

Chosen Woman 4: "Is there a way to cleanse and enhance the energy of the fabrics we wear?"

Woman Clothed with the Sun: "Yes. You can cleanse your fabrics with natural elements like sunlight, moonlight, and living water. Infuse them with your intentions and positive energy to enhance their vibrational qualities."

24: Universal Economics and the Song of the Elders

Woman Clothed with the Sun: "In the realm of Aka-Ra-Aka, our garments are not just for physical protection; they are sacred tools that interact with our energy fields. Be mindful of what you wear and how it influences your energy. Let your clothing reflect the light within you and support your journey towards balance and harmony."

The chosen women nod in understanding, their faces glowing with newfound knowledge. The session ends with a sense of unity and purpose, each woman ready to embrace the teachings and apply them in their lives.

Lila (thinking): *This has been an enlightening experience. I never realized how much the fabrics we wear can impact our energy. I'm excited to explore this further and see how it enhances my journey in Aka-Ra-Aka.

As they leave Ahia-Ka-Ala, the chosen women feel a renewed sense of connection to their garments, understanding their deeper significance and power.

Song | 23

Poetry of the Iroko tree

The Twenty-Third Song

Osisi Iroko—*Ahia Ka Ala*—Ụlọ Nsọ Dị Ndụ

N'*ime obi nke oke ohia, ebe onyinyo na-agba egwu,*

Na-eguzo Iroko, n'ọhụụ na-adịghị agwụ agwụ.

Giant nke ochie, nke nwere mgbọrọgwụ miri emi ma sie ike;

Ọ na-ahapụ ntanye nzuzo, abụ ochie.

N'okpuru alaka gị, ebe ìhè na-enwu enwu.

Mmụọ nke ndị nna nna na alaka gị na-egwu mmiri.

N'ichebe ala, ị na-agbachi nkịtị;

Ncheta na nrọ na ogbugbo gị miri emi.

Iroko, ogidi igwe,

24: Universal Economics and the Song of the Elders

Okpueze gị na-emetụ kpakpando aka, ka igwe ojii na-agafe.

Ọnụ ụzọ nke alaeze ebe Chineke bi,

Site n'osisi dị nsọ gị, ụwa na-agbakọ.

Site na mgbọrọgwụ gị ka ndụ si puta, ọgaranya dị ọcha;

Ọgwụgwọ na ike, n'ime isi gị na-atachi obi.

ogbugbo gị bụ ọta, gị na-ahapụ balm;

N'ihu gị, ụwa na-ahụ jụụ.

A kpara akụkọ ifo n'ụdị ị na-ebu,

Akụkọ banyere oge gara aga, ịhụnanya na obi nkoropụ.

Ndị ochie na-ekwu maka ike omimi gị;

Otu esi edozi ụwa, site n'ehihie ruo abalị.

Iroko, Iroko, mmụọ osisi,

Onye nche nzuzo, ọhịa na n'efu

24: Universal Economics and the Song of the Elders

Site n'oké ifufe, ị na-eguzo, na-adịghị eguzosi ike na eziokwu,

Akara nke ebighi-ebi, emeghariri ọhụrụ.

Ka anyị sọpụrụ ike gị, amara gị, ebube gị,

Ma zọọ ije n'ala efu, ruo mgbe ebighị ebi.

N'ihi na n'okpuru ndò gị, anyị na-achọta ụzọ anyị.

Ìhè nke ụbọchị ebighị ebi gị na-eduzi.

N'obi Enugu, ebe onyinyo gị dara,

Nkwughachi nke amamihe n'oku gị na-agbachi nkịtị.

Ị na-akụziri anyị ihe ziri ezi, udo na ìhè.

Nke ịdị n'otu na ọdịdị, ma ehihie na abalị.

Ah Iroko, dị nsọ na nnukwu,

Onye nchekwa mmụọ, ị nyere anyị aka ịghọta.

Nke ahụ dị mfe na nnabata nke okike,

Anyị na-ahụ Chineke, n'ebe a dị nsọ.

24: Universal Economics and the Song of the Elders

Iroko Tree—*The Living Ahia-Ka-Ala* (Temple)

In the heart of the forest, where shadows dance,

Stands the Iroko, in a timeless trance.

A giant of old, with roots deep and strong,

Its leaves whisper secrets, an ancient song.

Beneath your boughs, where the light is dim,

Spirits of ancestors in your branches swim.

Guarding the land, you silently keep,

Memories and dreams in your bark so deep.

Oh Iroko, pillar of the sky,

Your crown touches stars, as clouds drift by.

A portal to realms where the divine reside,

Through your sacred wood, worlds collide.

From your roots springs life, rich and pure,

24: Universal Economics and the Song of the Elders

Healing and strength, in your essence endure.

Your bark a shield, your leaves a balm,

In your presence, the world finds calm.

Legends are woven in the patterns you bear,

Tales of the past, of love and despair.

The old ones speak of your mystical might,

How you balance the worlds, from day into night.

Iroko, Iroko, spirit of the tree,

Guardian of secrets, wild and free.

Through storms you stand, unyielding and true,

A symbol of eternity, ever renewed.

May we honor your power, your grace, your lore,

And tread lightly on the earth, forevermore.

For in your shade, we find our way,

Guided by the light of your eternal day.

24: Universal Economics and the Song of the Elders

In Enugu's heart, where your shadow falls,

Echoes of wisdom in your silent calls.

You teach us of balance, of peace and light,

Of unity in nature, both day and night.

Oh Iroko, sacred and grand,

Protector of spirits, you help us understand.

That in simplicity and nature's embrace,

We find Chi na Aka, in this holy place.

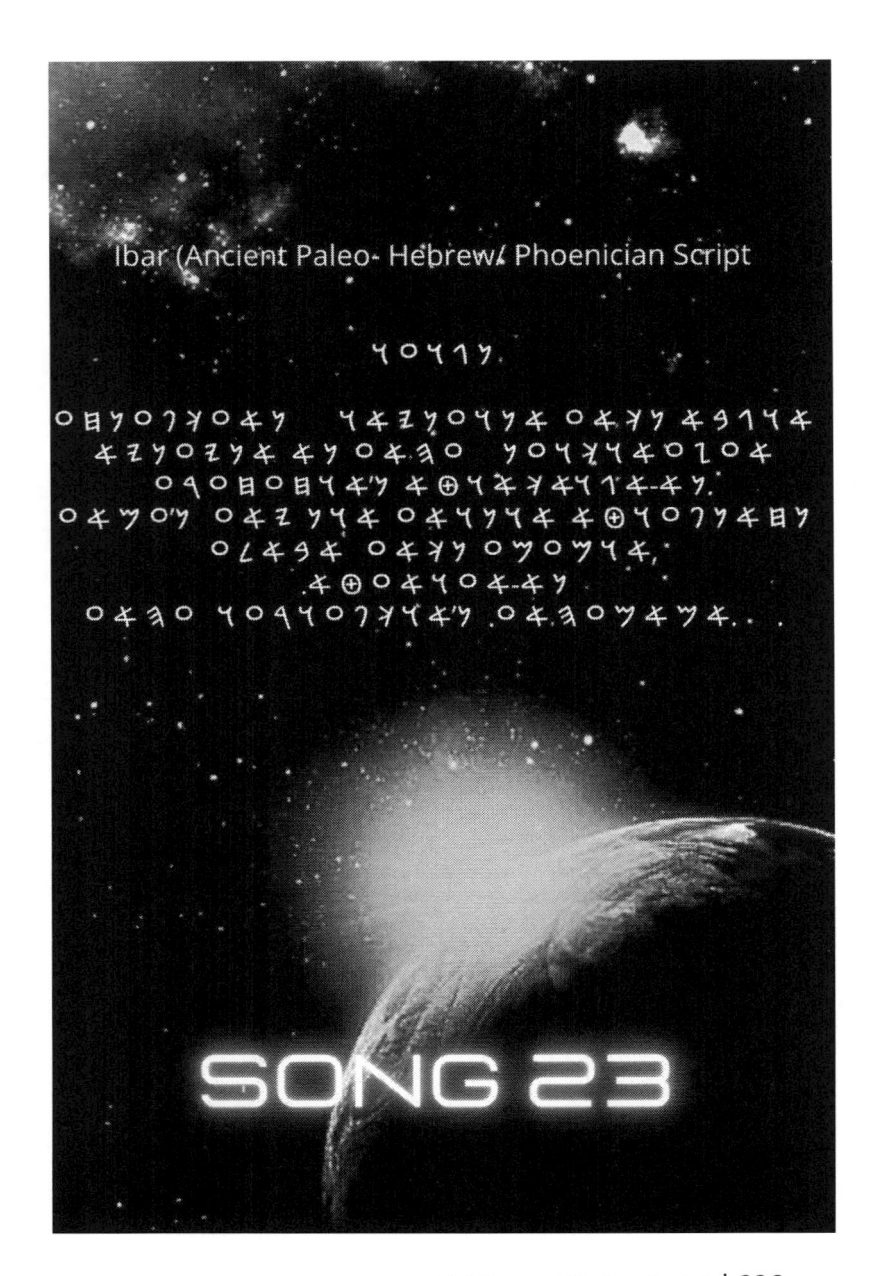

24: Universal Economics and the Song of the Elders

Ibar (Ancient Paleo-Hebrew/Phoenician Script)

SONG 23

Tai-Zamarai Yasharahyalah | 336

24: Universal Economics and the Song of the Elders

Transliteration

<u>Ngwiw</u>

Awgba nkai anyinyaw naikpiwchi aiziawkwiw; ihai na anyinya na-agwakawta n'awchichiri.

Nchawpiwta awnwai awnyai n'imai awmimi nkai abali,

Na-aiwaita amamihai n'awkpiwriw ihai.

Igbo Translation

<u>Ngwu</u>

Ọmịmị nke ụwa

Ọgba nke onyinyo nēkpuchi eziokwu;

Ìhè na onyinyo na-agwakọta n'ọchịchịrị.

Nchọpụta onwe onye n'ime omimi nke abalị,

Na-eweta amamihe n'okpuru ìhè.

English Translation:

<u>Ngwu</u>

Lower Terrestrial-Celestial Market Rises

The cavern of shadows hides truth,

Light and shadow blend in darkness.

Self-discovery in the depth of night,

Brings wisdom beneath the light.

24: Universal Economics and the Song of the Elders

Song | 24

The Sacred Iroko Tree

The 24th and Final Song

High Priestess Amina's Journey to the Past

Enugu, Ancient Times

High Priestess Amina stood in the exact location where her temple once stood, only to find herself surrounded by a verdant forest. In place of the sophisticated architecture, there now stood a grand Iroko tree, its branches stretching towards the heavens. A guide, shimmering with ethereal light, approached her.

Guide: "The divine powers do not dwell in temples made with hands. The Iroko tree governs the people of this land and serves as a portal to the 12th dimension. There are twelve such portals across the earth. Your task is to restore reverence for the Iroko tree in various regions of Africa, starting here in Enugu."

Amina absorbed her surroundings, witnessing the simplicity and serenity of the ancient Enugu people. They lived in huts made of clay and thatched roofs, their lifestyle centered around farming and

24: Universal Economics and the Song of the Elders

communal harmony. The men tilled the soil with ancient tools, while the women worked beside them, planting and harvesting crops.

24: Universal Economics and the Song of the Elders

Ibar (Ancient Paleo-Hebrew/ Phoenician Script)

SONG 24

24: Universal Economics and the Song of the Elders

Transliteration

<u>Ala Igwai</u>

Awchaiaizai nkai mgbai aibighi aibi na-aigiwzawsi ikai,

Aigwiw ikpaiaziw na-aikwiwghawchi na idi iwkwiwiw ya.

Idi n'awtiw nkai ihai niilai di n'iwwa,

Na-aichaitara anyi na anyi biw akiwkiw nkai aibighi aibi.

Igbo Translation

<u>Ala Igwe</u>

Ocheeze nke mgbe ebighị ebi na-eguzosi ike,

Egwu ikpeazụ na-ekwughachi na ịdị ukwuu ya.

Ịdị n'otu nke ihe niile dị n'ụwa,

Na-echetara anyị na anyị bụ akụkụ nke ebighi ebi.

24: Universal Economics and the Song of the Elders

English Translation:

Awala (Paradise)

The throne of eternity stands firm,

The final song echoes in its grandeur.

Unity of all things in the world,

Reminds us we are part of eternity.

Daily Life in Ancient Enugu

Ancient Enugu Village

The villagers wore simple, loose clothing made of raw pure linen, woven with care and dyed in natural hues. Their days began with the sun's first light and ended with the setting sun.

Village Elder: "Every animal is sacred, Iwa-aya. We do not hunt or sacrifice them. Instead, we live in harmony, acknowledging the interconnectedness of all life."

Children ran barefoot, their laughter mingling with the sounds of nature. The village thrived on trade, exchanging crops, handcrafted goods, and woven fabrics with neighboring communities.

Guide: "Do you notice the linen loose clothing they are wearing, it carries the essence of our land and spirit. Wearing it feels like being wrapped in the embrace of our ancestors."

The People of Bayelsa

Ancient Bayelsa Region

In Bayelsa, the lifestyle was similar yet distinct. The Ijaw people lived by the rivers, their huts built on stilts to protect against floods. They were skilled fishermen, their canoes slicing through the water with ease. The community revered the water as much as the land, seeing it as a source of life and sustenance.

River-Dwellers: "The river is our mother. She provides for us, and we respect her by taking only what we need. We do not hunt any living thing in the river, we consider them all our family. Only seaweed, corals, pearls, and anything our mother offers to us"

Their clothing was also made of linen, adapted for their humid environment. Trade here involved shells, salt and woven goods, fostering a strong connection with other coastal communities.

24: Universal Economics and the Song of the Elders

The Ekiti People

Ancient Ekiti Region

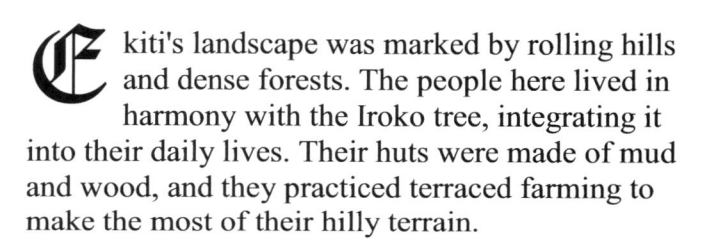

Ekiti's landscape was marked by rolling hills and dense forests. The people here lived in harmony with the Iroko tree, integrating it into their daily lives. Their huts were made of mud and wood, and they practiced terraced farming to make the most of their hilly terrain.

Villager: "The Iroko tree is sacred. It stands as a guardian, a bridge between our world and the divine."

The Legal Battle

Modern Ekiti, Courtroom

The battles to save an ancient Iroko tree in Ekiti had reached the courtroom. High Priestess Amina, empowered by the elders, stood alongside environmental activists and community leaders.

Lawyer for the Defense: "Your honor, this tree is not just any tree. It is a sacred symbol, integral to the cultural and spiritual identity of the Ekiti people."

The opposing counsel, representing developers, argued for progress and modernization, but the

24: Universal Economics and the Song of the Elders

courtroom buzzed with a sense of urgency to preserve tradition and natural heritage.

Judge: "We must weigh the importance of cultural heritage against economic development. This is a decision that affects not just the land, but the soul of the people."

Dialogue Among the 24 Elders

Council Chamber in the 12th Dimension

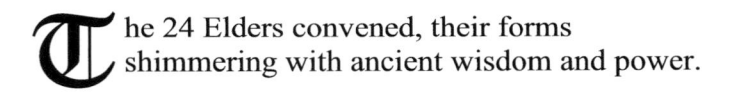

The 24 Elders convened, their forms shimmering with ancient wisdom and power.

Elder Wadana: "Amina faces great challenges. The balance of the realms depends on the reverence of the Iroko tree."

Elder Amammaw: "We must provide her with the knowledge and support she needs. The consequences of failure are dire."

Elder Nnlanari: "She is strong and determined. With our guidance, she will succeed."

They discussed strategies to assist Amina, from sending visions to influencing key individuals who could aid her mission. The fate of the Iroko tree, and the balance of the realms, lay in their collective hands.

24: Universal Economics and the Song of the Elders

The Spiritual Battle

Ekiti Forest

High Priestess Amina stood before the ancient Iroko tree, feeling its power and presence. She began a ritual, calling upon the spirits of the land and the wisdom of the elders.

Amina: "Great Iroko, guardian of the realms, we seek your strength and guidance. Protect this sacred tree from harm."

The forest came alive with energy, the air thick with anticipation. The ritual was a profound act of reverence, intended to awaken the spirits and rally them to the cause.

The Iroko Tree's Power

Enugu, Present Day

Back in her temple, Amina reflected on her journey and the significance of the Iroko tree. The tree's healing and protective qualities, its role in connecting the human and spiritual realms, had been made clear. She was determined to restore its reverence, starting with her own community.

24: Universal Economics and the Song of the Elders

Amina: "The Iroko tree is our link to the divine, our protector, and our healer. We must honor it and ensure its legacy for future generations."

The High Priestess Amina's journey emphasizes the profound connection between nature, spirituality, and cultural heritage. The sacred Iroko tree stands as a testament to this connection, embodying the wisdom and strength of ancient traditions that continue to guide and protect humanity. The Iroko tree governs it people in present time and for all eternity.

Daily Life in Ancient Enugu Continued

Enugu Village, Ancient Times

High Priestess Amina found herself amidst the bustling life of an ancient Enugu village. The guide, still shimmering with ethereal light, walked beside her, explaining the significance of what she was witnessing.

Guide: "Look around, Amina. This is how your ancestors lived, in harmony with nature. Their huts are simple, made of clay and thatch. Their lives are intertwined with the land and its rhythms. Everything they do, from farming to trading, is guided by a deep respect for the earth and all its inhabitants."

24: Universal Economics and the Song of the Elders

Amina observed the villagers as they went about their daily routines. Men tilled the soil, their bodies moving in a synchronized dance with the earth. Women worked beside them, planting seeds and tending to crops. The community was vibrant, full of life and laughter.

Guide: "They wear loose clothing made of raw pure linen, woven with care. Linen is not just a fabric to them; it is a symbol of purity and connection to the divine. It breathes with the body, allowing the flow of energy, and is believed to carry the essence of the land and spirit. This simplicity and oneness with nature are what you must restore in your time."

The scene shifted to the village river, where two maidens were fetching water. They carried earthen vessels on their heads, filled with the cool, clear water of the community river.

Nwanyị Otu: (ịchị ọchị) "Adanna, ị hụla Chike taa? Ọ nọ n'ahịa mbụ, echere m na ọ lere m anya."

Maiden 1: (smiling) "Adanna, have you seen Chike today? He was at the market earlier, and I think he looked at me."

Nwa agbọghọ abuo: (na-achị ọchị) "Ah, Chidinma, ị na-echekarị na ụmụ nwoke na-ele gị anya. mana ee, ahụrụ m ya. Ọ mara mma nke ukwuu, ọ bụghị ya? Ike na obiọma."

Maiden 2: (laughing) "Oh, Chidinma, you always think the boys are looking at you. But yes, I saw him. He is very handsome, isn't he? Strong and kind."

Nwanyị Otu: "Ee, nne ya sịkwa na ọ bụ ezigbo onye ọrụ ugbo. Nne m sị ezigbo onye ọrụ ugbo na-eme ezigbo di."

Maiden 1: "Yes, and his mother says he is a good farmer. My mother says a good farmer makes a good husband."

Nwa agbọghọ abụọ: "Ee, anyị ga-ahụ. Nshimirii - Chi osimiri nwere ike nwee atụmatụ maka gị abụọ."

Maiden 2: "Well, we shall see. Nshimirii—The river diety might have plans for you both."

They laughed, their voices blending with the sound of the flowing river and the rustling leaves of the Iroko tree nearby.

Guide: "Do you see, Amina? Their lives are simple, yet full of joy and meaning. They are connected to each other and the land. Their interactions, their clothing, their way of life—all are expressions of a deeper spiritual truth. The Iroko tree stands as a guardian, a portal to the divine, just as it does now.

24: Universal Economics and the Song of the Elders

But the reverence for such natural elements has diminished in your time."

Amina felt a deep sense of awe and responsibility. She understood the importance of the guide's words and the vision she was shown.

Amina: "I see now. The simplicity of their lives, their connection to nature, and the spiritual significance of linen—these are the keys to restoring balance. I will do all I can to revive this way of life, starting in Enugu."

Guide: "You have been chosen for this task because of your wisdom and strength. Remember, the Iroko tree is not just a symbol, but a living testament to the harmony between the human and the divine. Honor it, and you will honor your ancestors and protect the future."

With these words, Amina felt a renewed sense of purpose. She knew her journey would be challenging, but she was ready to embrace it, armed with the wisdom of her ancestors and the support of the 24 Elders.

24: Universal Economics and the Song of the Elders

Epilogue

United by the Song

The Infinite Journey

The world has been restored to balance, thanks to the efforts of scientists, spiritual leaders, and common people united by the songs of the Elders. Priestess Amina and her initiates continue their spiritual work, guiding humanity towards a brighter, harmonious future.

Setting

An ethereal realm, a convergence point of the 12 dimensions. This realm is a place of pure light and no shadows, where the boundaries of reality blur. The sky is a swirling tapestry of colors, and the ground beneath glows with an otherworldly luminescence. Its atmosphere is charged with cosmic energy, creating a sense of awe and wonder.

Portal Transition: A dynamic and vibrant passageway that connects the ethereal realm to the physical world, symbolizing the connection between dimensions and the journey of the soul.

24: Universal Economics and the Song of the Elders

The Custodian stands at the center of the ethereal realm, surrounded by the Chosen Individuals and Higher Beings. The air is thick with the hum of cosmic energy.

The Custodian: "You have journeyed through the realms of possibility, faced challenges, and discovered the power within you. The 12 dimensions are vast, each with its own mysteries and truths."

The Chosen Individuals, each representing their region, look around in awe. They feel the weight of their experiences and the significance of their journey.

The Custodian: "From the ancient stones of Stonehenge to the bustling streets of New York City, from the serene hills of Arkansas to the futuristic city of Awala, you have seen the diverse facets of existence. You have learned the importance of balance, love, persistence, and hope."

Ahia Aya | Ah (Higher Being 1): "The universe is a tapestry woven from the threads of countless lives and dimensions. Each thread is crucial, each life significant."

Ahia Aya | Ba (Higher Being 2): "Your actions have ripple effects, touching lives across dimensions. You are more than travelers; you are creators of your destiny."

24: Universal Economics and the Song of the Elders

The Custodian: "As custodians of knowledge and bearers of light, your journey does not end here. It is but a chapter in the infinite book of existence. You will return to your worlds, but now you carry the wisdom of the cosmos within you."

The Chosen Individuals exchange looks of understanding and determination. They feel the empowerment that comes from their shared experiences.

The Custodian: "Remember the declaration you made: 'I am a traveler. I choose to travel the unknown. I know the infinite possibilities and risks. I am pure of heart. I trust the process. I trust. I am.'"

The realm around them begins to shift, the colors intensifying and the energy growing. The Custodian raises their hands, and a portal opens.

The Custodian: "Go forth, and continue your journey. The 12 dimensions are always within you. Trust the process, trust yourselves, and know that you are never alone."

One by one, the Chosen Individuals step through the portal, each returning to their respective regions on Earth. They carry with them the knowledge and wisdom they have gained, ready to apply it to their lives and inspire others.

24: Universal Economics and the Song of the Elders

The Continuing Journey

Narrator: "The cosmic songs continue to resonate, reminding us of the interconnectedness of all life. As Adora and her initiates lead the way, the message is clear: the true power lies in the unity of the heart and the purity of our intentions."

Song 4

Decoded: "In the unity of hearts, the cosmos finds peace. Embrace this truth, and let it guide your path."

Narrator: "And so, the journey of the heart continues, with each step bringing us closer to the harmonious balance of the cosmos."

The Chosen Individuals comes to a full circle, emphasizing the interconnectedness of the 12 dimensions and the infinite nature of their journey. The Custodian, along with Ahia Aya (Higher Beings), imparts final wisdom, highlighting the significance of balance, love, persistence, and faith. The Chosen Individuals, empowered by their experiences, return to their respective regions on Earth, ready to apply their newfound knowledge inspiring others in growth and exploration; in a sense of wonder, and to continuously seek out the infinite possibilities within their own lives.

24: Universal Economics and the Song of the Elders

Appendices

Character Profiles

Prologue

- **The Architect**: The primary founder and creator of the 12th Realm.

- **The Luminary**: A being of immense wisdom, co-creator of the realm.

- **The Herald**: The announcer of decrees and laws.

- **The Custodian**: The guardian and overseer of the 12 realms.

- **Dr. Alara Tanis**: A renowned quantum physicist.

- **Dr. Jean-Luc Dubois**: A Swiss physicist.

- **Dr. Mei Wang**: A Chinese physicist visiting from Southeast China.

- **High Priestess Amina**: The leader of the custodians.

24: Universal Economics and the Song of the Elders

- **Initiates**: A group of chosen individuals from different parts of the world.

- **Elder Shamar**: A wise and elderly custodian.

- **Zam Zam**: A young initiate from Peckham, London.

- **President Lumumba**: The charismatic leader of the assembly.

- **Delegates**: Representatives from Switzerland, the UK, China, Honduras, Nigeria, Kenya, Gambia, Guinea-Bissau, the US, and other regions.

- **Trader Kofi:** A merchant dealing in interstellar goods.

- **Mari**: A local woman curious about the market.

Song 1

- **Dr. Alara Tanis**: A renowned quantum physicist.

24: Universal Economics and the Song of the Elders

- **Professor Marcus Sloane**: A theoretical physicist.

- **Dr. Jean-Luc Dubois**: A Swiss physicist.

- **Dr. Mei Wang**: A Chinese physicist visiting from Southeast China.

- **Ida Ala-Amin**: A research assistant.

- **AI Voice (ALPHA):** The lab's AI system.

Elder Mmbagwiw, the Keeper of Light, has an appearance that embodies purity and brightness. Her form is enveloped in a robe of shimmering white, and her eyes shine with a golden light that speaks of ages of knowledge.

- **Elder Zaphyr Nkwa**, the Master of Winds, appears as a translucent figure, constantly shifting like a gentle breeze. His voice carries the whisper of the wind, calm and soothing.

- **Elder Zaphyr Nnshimiri,** the Guardian of Oceans, has a form that seems to flow like water, her robes undulating in waves of deep blue and green. Her presence brings a sense of tranquility and depth.

- **Elder Zaphyr Abaraka**, the Wielder of Flames, radiates warmth and energy. His form is a blaze of

24: Universal Economics and the Song of the Elders

fiery hues, and his eyes burn with an intensity that can be both comforting and intimidating.

- **Elder Akachi:** The leader of the Elders.

- **Elder Zamarachi:** A gentle and wise Elder.

- **Elder Amadiahia:** A stern and powerful Elder.

- **Ala (The Woman Clothed with the Sun)**: A powerful and enigmatic figure.

- **Lila**: A mortal chosen to visit Aka Ra Aka.

- **Addida (Fate Weaver):** A being who manipulates the threads of destiny.

- **The Call:** Etheral Voice

- **Nyah Kimani**: Chosen Initiate from Kenya

- **Nyah Kimani's Grandmother (in Kikuyu):** A wise nurturing elder.

24: Universal Economics and the Song of the Elders

- **Dr. Lucas Bern:** Head of Engineering.

- **Anya Müller:** Research assistant.

- **Marc:** A local artist and friend of the team.

- **Chisom:** A barista who knows the team well.

- **Mei's Niece:** A playful, happy 4 yr old

Song 2

- **Local Scholar** in southeastern China

Elder Mmbagwiw, the Keeper of Light:

- *Origin:* Mmbagwiw was a being of pure light, born from the first dawn of the multiverse. Her wisdom and purity made her a natural leader among the realms of light.

- *Responsibilities:* Mmbagwiw oversees all matters of illumination and enlightenment. She ensures that the light of knowledge and truth permeates throughout the dimensions, guiding beings towards higher understanding and harmony.

24: Universal Economics and the Song of the Elders

- **Dr. Alara Tanis**: Quantum physicist.

- **Dr. Jean-Luc Dubois**: Swiss physicist.

- **Ida Ala-Amin**: Research assistant.

- **Lila:** A mortal chosen to visit Aka Ra Aka.

- **Ala (The Woman Clothed with the Sun):** Guardian of the realm.

- **Addida (Fate Weaver):** A being who manipulates the threads of destiny.

- **Zam Zam:** Young initiate from Peckham.

- **Amma:** Zam Zam's childhood friend.

- **Mysterious Stranger:** A guide sent by the Elders.

- **Chimamanda:** A local woman with a mysterious past.

- **Trader Kofi:** A merchant dealing in interstellar goods.

24: Universal Economics and the Song of the Elders

- **High Priestess Amina:** Leader of the custodians.

- **Priestess Amina, her initiates, local villagers**

- **Dr. Alara Tanis:** Quantum physicist.

- **Dr. Jean-Luc Dubois:** Swiss physicist.

- **Ida Al-Amin:** Research assistant.

- **Dr. Mei Wang:** Chinese physicist (via video call).

- **Professor Anton Petrova:** Russian physicist.

- **President Lumumba:** Leader of the assembly.

- **Delegates:** Representatives from various regions.

- **Chimamanda:** A chosen custodian.

- **Trader Kofi:** A merchant dealing in interstellar goods.

- **Local Buyer:** A curious customer.

24: Universal Economics and the Song of the Elders

- **High Priestess Amina:** Leader of the custodians.

- **Elder Amadiahia:** One of the 24 Elders, responsible for overseeing the creation process.

- **Elder Achichi:** Another Elder, focused on the balance of energy across the multiverse.

- **Cosmic Observers:** Beings who monitor the events in various dimensions.

- **Mwende:** Initiate

- **Mama Mwende:** Mwende's mother

- **Kijana:** A local elder guiding Mwende.

Song 4

- **Kenyan initiate, local shamans**

- **Dr. Mei Wang:** Chinese physicist.

24: Universal Economics and the Song of the Elders

- **Liang:** A monk and spiritual guide.

- **Yara:** A young woman seeking answers.

- **Dr. Jean-Luc Dubois:** Swiss physicist.

- **Ida Ala-Amin:** Research assistant.

- **Dr. Alara Tanis:** Quantum physicist.

- **Professor Anton Petrova:** Russian physicist.

- **Dr. Alara Tanis:** Quantum physicist.

- **Dr. Jean-Luc Dubois:** Swiss physicist.

- **Ida Ala-Amin:** Research assistant.

- **Dr. Mei Wang:** Chinese physicist (via video call).

- **Elder Saraphina:** Guardian of soul creation.

- **Soul Architect:** A being responsible for designing new souls.

- **Young Souls:** Newly created souls ready to embark on their journeys.

24: Universal Economics and the Song of the Elders

- **Elder Saraphina**

- **Elder Mmbagwiw**

- **Cosmic Economists**

- **Dr. Alara Tanis**

- **Anya Müller**

- **Dr. Lucas Bern**

Song 5

- **Lila:** A mortal navigating the Abyss.

- **The Gatekeeper:** A guardian of the Abyss.

- **Reverberations of the Past:** Manifestations of Lila's past thoughts and actions.

- **Chimamanda:** A chosen custodian, now back on Earth.

- **Sefu:** A local youth.

24: Universal Economics and the Song of the Elders

- **Elder Mbala:** A wise elder who understands the multiverse.

- **Zam Zam :** Young initiate.

- **Amma:** Zam Zam's childhood friend.

- **Dr. Awana Mitchell:** A scientist who studies human behavior from an interstellar perspective.

- **Elder Wariamn:** Overseer of the Twelve Layers of Hell.

- **Lost Soul:** A soul caught in the cycle of negative actions and thoughts.

- **Guide:** A being tasked with guiding souls through their trials.

- **Wandering Souls:** Souls stumbling unable to find a clear path

- **Artificial Overseers:** Overseers of the sixth layer of Hell where humans are treated as arttificial intelligence, only capable of processing data and following prompts

24: Universal Economics and the Song of the Elders

- **Addida:** A race of cosmic spiders in the ninth layer of Hell

---

- **Dr. Alara Tanis**

- **Dr. Lucas Bern**

- **Anya Müller**

- **Mwende**

- **Mama Mwende**

- **Kijana**

Song 6

- **Dr. Alara Tanis:** Quantum physicist.

- **Arach:** Leader of the Addida, the cosmic spider race.

- **Ida Ala-Amin:** Research assistant.

24: Universal Economics and the Song of the Elders

- **Trader Kofi:** A merchant dealing in interstellar goods.

- **Sergeant Rodriguez:** A local law enforcer.

- **Mysterious Stranger:** A shadowy figure with a hidden agenda.

- **President Lumumba:** Leader of the assembly.

- **Chimamanda:** A chosen custodian.

- **Delegates:** Representatives from various regions.

- **Dr. Jean-Luc Dubois:** Swiss physicist.

- **Dr. Alara Tanis:** Quantum physicist.

- **Ida Ala-Amin:** Research assistant.

- **Dr. Mei Wang:** Chinese physicist (via video call).

- **The Cosmic Spider Race:** Addida

- **Elder Wariamn:** Chair of the Cosmic Council.

- **Addida Leader**

24: Universal Economics and the Song of the Elders

- **Dr. Alara Tanis:** Earth representative.

- **Interstellar Delegates**

- **Interstellar Delegates**

- **Local Enforcers**

- **Elder Wariamn**

- **Dr. Alara Tanis**

- **Chimamanda:** A chosen custodian.

- **Elder Mbala:** A wise elder.

- **Community Members:** Diverse group from Kinshasa.

- **Dr. Mei Wang:** Chinese physicist.

- **Liang:** A monk and spiritual guide.

- **Yara:** A young woman seeking answers.

24: Universal Economics and the Song of the Elders

- **Dr. Amara Harris:** Neuroscientist.

- **Professor Isaac Cohen:** Theoretical physicist.

- **Dr. Amina Patel:** Cognitive psychologist.

- **Zam Zam:** Young initiate.

- **Amma:** Zam Zam's childhood friend.

- **Marcus:** A paranoid survivalist.

- **Dr. Sham Carter:** Disaster management expert.

- **Laura Matthews:** A survivor.

- **Officer Hernandez:** A local police officer.

- **Dr. Alara Tanis**

- **Local Leaders**

- **Survivors**

24: Universal Economics and the Song of the Elders

Song 7

- **Chimamanda:** A chosen custodian.

- **Elder Mbala:** A wise elder.

- **Community Members:** Diverse group from Kinshasa.

- **Dr. Mei Wang:** Chinese physicist.

- **Liang:** A monk and spiritual guide.

- **Yara:** A young woman seeking answers.

Song 8

- **Zam Zam:** Young initiate.

- **Amma:** Zam Zam's childhood friend.

- **Marcus:** A paranoid survivalist.

Officer Hernandez, Dr. Carter, Laura: Trio searching for survivors in the aftermath of a disaster caused by a dimensional rift.

24: Universal Economics and the Song of the Elders

Song 9

- **Mwangi:** A local shopkeeper

- **Amina:** A hopeful young woman.

- **Kariuki:** A disillusioned elder

- **Dr. Mei Wang:** Chinese physicist.

- **Liang:** A monk and spiritual guide.

- **Yara:** A young woman seeking answers.

- **Adama:** A fisherman.

- **Fatou:** Adama's wife.

- **Nia:** Their daughter.

- **Dr. Alara Tanis**

- **Dr. Lucas Bern**

- **Dr. Mei Wang** *(via video call)*

24: Universal Economics and the Song of the Elders

- **Research Team Members**

- **High Priestess Amina**
- **Local Villagers**
- **Chidi:** A young villager seeking guidance.

- **Adama**
- **Elder Kito:** A respected elder in the community.
- **Local Youths**

- **Elder Wariamn**
- **Dr. Alara Tanis**
- **High Priestess Amina**
- **Archivist Zara**
- **Adama:** A young initiate from Kenya.

24: Universal Economics and the Song of the Elders

Song 9

- **Chinwe:** An artist.

- **Amara:** Chinwe's assistant.

- **Kelechi:** A visitor and art enthusiast.

- **High Priestess Amina**

- **Chidi**

- **Local Villagers**

- **Dr. Hans Müller:** Geneticist.

- **Lena:** Research assistant.

- **Johann:** A subject of their study.

- **Dr. Lucas Bern, Dr. Alara Tanis, Research Team Member:** In the genetics lab at CERN, studying the effects of biological manipulation on human perception.

24: Universal Economics and the Song of the Elders

- **Adama, Elder Kito, Local Youths:** Walking through the Maasai Mara, discussing the difference between real and imagined experiences.

- **Claire:** A writer.

- **David:** Claire's friend.

- **Anna:** A local resident.

- **Dr. Alara Tanis, High Priestess Amina, Adama, Community Leaders, Local Residents:** In various locations on Earth, simultaneously address the question of why certain groups face hatred and prejudice.

Song 11

- **Amaka:** A young environmental activist.

- **Nwabungwu:** Emily's mentor and a seasoned environmentalist.

- **Tamara:** A local farmer.

24: Universal Economics and the Song of the Elders

- **Dr. Carlos Martinez:** Lead scientist.

- **Sofia:** Data analyst.

- **Nila:** A tech-savvy intern.

- **Mama Nkechi:** The matriarch of the family.

- **Obi:** Her eldest son.

- **Zuri:** Obi's wife.

Song 12

- **Abena:** A spiritual guide.

- **Kwame:** A seeker of wisdom.

- **Nia:** Kwame's daughter.

- **Dr. Isa Mbemba:** Surgeon.

- **Dani:** A patient recovering from surgery.

- **Marta:** Daniel's wife.

24: Universal Economics and the Song of the Elders

- **Wei:** A young entrepreneur.

- **Li Mei:** Wei's business partner.

- **Chen:** A local shopkeeper.

Song 13

- **Alana:** An astrophysicist.

- **Thomas:** A historian.

- **Lila:** Alana's niece, a curious teenager.

- **Captain Marcus Farah:** Leader of the space mission.

- **Dr. Aisha Khan:** A biologist.

- **Lieutenant Tai Chawan:** An engineer.

- **Dr. Sarah Johnson:** Geneticist.

- **Iwah:** A young researcher.

- **Maya:** A visiting scholar.

24: Universal Economics and the Song of the Elders

- **Dr. Jean-Luc Dubois, Dr. Mei Wang, Dr. Alara Tanis, Priestess Amina, Global Leaders:** Global leaders unite with scientists and spiritual leaders to restore balance.

Song 14

- **Dr. Farah Ala-Shalah:** An archaeologist.

- **Nnam:** A local guide.

- **Nadine:** A researcher in ancient cultures.

- **Alex:** A financial advisor.

- **Jasmine:** A young entrepreneur.

- **Athan:** A life coach.

- **Mila:** A city planner.

- **Yanah:** A sustainability expert.

- **Arla:** A technology developer.

24: Universal Economics and the Song of the Elders

Song 15

- **Dr. Ayomide Ibrahim:** A Nigerian anthropologist and priestess.

- **Dr. Nyah Kimani:** A Kenyan biologist and initiate in the ancient temple.

- **Dr. Carlos Mendoza:** A Brazilian engineer working at CERN.

- **Dr. Hiroshi Nakamura:** A Japanese astrophysicist and expert in quantum mechanics.

- **Dr. Anya Petrov:** A Russian mathematician specializing in theoretical physics.

- **Nyah Kimani:** a dedicated environmental activist who shares her passion for sustainable development and cultural preservation.

- **Priestess Amina**: A wise and eloquent spiritual guide

- **Christian:** A passionate 'believer'.

- **Passersby:** villagers, visitors.

24: Universal Economics and the Song of the Elders

Song 16

- **Priestess Amina:** The head priestess, known for her wisdom and compassion.

- **Nneka:** A young local woman who often helps at the temple.

- **Ifeanyi:** An elder from the nearby village.

- **Local Villagers:** Regular visitors to the temple.

- **Mwende:** A young initiate preparing for her journey.

- **Mama Mwende:** Mwende's mother.

- **Kijana:** A local elder guiding Mwende.

Song 17-18

- **Dr. Carlos Mendoza:** Works on a complex engineering project at CERN

- **Dr. Hiroshi Nakamura:** Grew up in Kyoto, Japan, steeped in the traditions of Zen Buddhism.

24: Universal Economics and the Song of the Elders

His parents were scientists, encouraging his fascination with the stars

- **Dr. Anya Petrov:** Was raised in Moscow, Russia, in a family of mathematicians and philosophers.

- **Dr. Ayomide Ibrahim:** *H*er *s*piritual beliefs are deeply rooted in Yoruba cosmology, which sees the universe as a balanced interplay of forces.

Song 19-24

- **Dr. Jean-Luc Dubois:** Swiss physicist.

- **Dr. Alara Tanis:** Quantum physicist.

- **Dr. Mei Wang:** Chinese physicist

- **Adora:** Initiate from Peckam

- **Johnathan:** Representative from the City of London.

Epilogue

- **The Custodian:** The guardian of the 12 dimensions.

- **Chosen Individuals:** Representatives from the 12 main regions on Earth.

- **Higher Beings:** Entities that exist beyond human comprehension, guiding and observing.

Appendix | A

The 24 Realms and Their Attributes

1. Realm of Balance and Order

- *Attributes*: Harmony, justice, equilibrium

- *Elder*: Achichi

2. Realm of Knowledge and Wisdom

- *Attributes*: Insight, enlightenment, understanding

- *Elder*: Alara

3. Realm of Life and Souls

- *Attributes:* Vitality, compassion, nurturing

- *Elder:* Saraphina

4. Realm of Transformation and Evolution

- *Attributes*: Change, adaptability, growth

- *Elder*: Nnaka

5. Realm of Light

- *Attributes:* Purity, clarity, illumination

- *Elder:* Mmbagwiw

6. Realm of Darkness

- *Attributes:* Mystery, potential, protection

- *Elder:* Amachichiri

7. Realm of Elements

- *Attributes:* Ahphar (Earth), Ahrayah (Water) Aka (Fire), Nkwa (Air)

- *Elder:* Zaphyr

8. Realm of Time

- *Attributes:* Continuity, cycles, history

- *Elder:* Mmgbar

9. Realm of Space

- *Attributes:* Infinity, dimension, structure

24: Universal Economics and the Song of the Elders

- *Elder:* Nnaga

10. Realm of Dreams

- *Attributes:* Imagination, subconscious, visions

- *Elder:* Mmata

11. Realm of Emotions

- *Attributes:* Passion, empathy, connection

- *Elder:* Mmatachi

12. Realm of Spirits

- *Attributes:* Essence, ethereality, transcendence

- *Elder:* Alammaw

13. Realm of Energy

- *Attributes:* Force, dynamism, vitality

- *Elder:* Amadiahia

14. Realm of Sound

24: Universal Economics and the Song of the Elders

- *Attributes:* Vibration, resonance, harmony

- *Elder:* Ikwiwghachi

15. Realm of Light and Shadow

- *Attributes:* Duality, balance, interplay

- *Elder:* Akachi

16. Realm of Flora

- *Attributes:* Growth, renewal, abundance

- *Elder:* Wadana

17. Realm of Fauna

- *Attributes:* Instinct, diversity, survival

- *Elder:* Nnlanari

18. Realm of Mind

- *Attributes:* Thought, intellect, consciousness

- *Elder:* Amamihia

19. Realm of Body

- *Attributes:* Strength, health, physicality

- *Elder:* Amaka

20. Realm of Technology

- *Attributes:* Innovation, machinery, advancement

- *Elder:* Taknnalanaza

21. Realm of Art

- *Attributes:* Creativity, expression, beauty

- *Elder:* Nnaichi

22. Realm of Law

- *Attributes:* Order, regulation, governance

- *Elder:* Tazadaaka

23. Realm of Love

- *Attributes:* Affection, unity, selflessness

- *Elder:* Zamarachi

24. Realm of War

- *Attributes:* Conflict, strategy, resolution

- *Elder:* Akwansa

Appendix | B

Terminology and Concepts

1. Cosmic Balance

- The equilibrium of forces across the multiverse maintained by the Elders.

2. Multiverse

- The entirety of all dimensions, realms, and universes.

3. Quantum Entanglement

- A phenomenon where particles remain interconnected, influencing each other regardless of distance.

4. Superposition

- A principle of quantum theory where particles exist in multiple states simultaneously.

5. Split Personality Deficiency Syndrome (SPDS)

- A condition caused by quantum disturbances leading to fragmented identities.

6. Interdimensional Travel

- The act of moving between different dimensions or realms.

7. Ethereal Beings

- Higher-dimensional entities interacting with the Elders.

8. Chamber of Prophecy

- A sacred space where Elders interpret cosmic prophecies.

9. Hall of Remembrance

- A memorial hall honoring past Elders and preserving their legacies.

10. Celestial Observatory

- A vantage point for observing cosmic phenomena and interacting with higher beings.

24: Universal Economics and the Song of the Elders

11. Gbiwrigbiwriw Cluster

- A barred soiral galaxy, the nearest major galaxy to the milky way. It is most prominent during Ahrayah (autumn) evenings in the Northern Hemisphere. Due to itsnorthern declination, Gbiwriwgbiwriw is visible only north of 40° south latitudes, as observed farther south. It lies below the horizon, and is considered one of the largest constellations, with an area of 722 square degrees. This is over 1,440 times the size of the moon.

12. Large Hadron Collider (LHC)

- The earth's largest and most powerful particle accelerator. It consists of a 27-kilometre ring of superconducting magnets with a number of accelerating structures to boost the energy of the particles along the way.

Appendix | C

The Structure and Hierarchy of the Council

1. *The Grand Elder*

- Presides over the council meetings, ensuring order and guiding discussions.

2. *High Elders*

- Senior members with additional responsibilities and decision-making authority.

3. *Junior Elders*

- Newly appointed or less experienced members, often in training for higher responsibilities.

4. *Advisory Committees*

- Specialized groups formed to address specific issues within the council's jurisdiction.

5. *Intergalactic Investigative and Enforcement Unit*

- A task force assigned to investigate and rectify major interdimensional disruptions.

6. *The Luminaries*

24: Universal Economics and the Song of the Elders

- Celestial entities, known to emanate an aura of infinite wisdom and compassion,

---

Index

A

- Adaptability (Realm of Transformation, Song 8)

- Ahlap-Bayath (Ancient-Hebrew alphabet)

Ah, Ba, Ga, Da, Ha, Wa, Za, Chaa, Ta, Ya, Ka, La, Ma, Na, Sa, I, Pa, Taza, Qa, Ra, Sha, Tha (*22 letters of the Ibar Ahlap-Bayath also used for numbering in multiples of 22 i.e 1-Ah; 2-Ba...22 Tha*)

- Ahia Aya (Literally transliterated '*Our Business*'; Collectively '*I am*')

- Akachi (Elder of Light and Shadow, Appendix A)

- Akwansa (Elder of War, Appendix A)

- Alammaw (Elder of Spirits, Appendix A)

- Alara (Elder of Knowledge, Appendix A)

- Amachichiri (Elder of Darkness, Appendix A)

- Amadiahia (Elder of Energy, Appendix A)

- Amaka (Elder of Body, Appendix A)

- Amamihia (Elder of Mind, Appendix A)

24: Universal Economics and the Song of the Elders

- Archives (Ancestral Archives, Song 2)

- Azira (Commander of the Unit, Appendix A)

B

- Balance (Cosmic Balance, Appendix B)

- Balance Chamber (Song 9)

C

- Celestial Beings (Interactions, Song 4)

- Celestial Observatory (Song 4)

- Con-CERNs (Song 11)

- Council of Elders (Introduction, Song 1)

- Council Meetings (Song 3)

- Cotton (Natural Fabric, Appendix B)

D

Dimension (See inter- Dimensional Travel Appendix B)

24: Universal Economics and the Song of the Elders

E

- Elders' Origins (Song 2)

- Elders' Responsibilities (Song 2)

- Elders' Sanctuaries (Song 5)

F

- Fate Weaver (Character, Appendix A)

- Flax (Historical Use, Appendix B)

- Flora (Realm of Flora, Appendix A)

G

- Geneva Citizen (Character)

- Grand Elder (Council Hierarchy, Appendix C)

- Great Hall of Justice (Song 3)

H

- Hall of Remembrance (Song 10)

- Healing Properties (Fabric, Appendix B)

24: Universal Economics and the Song of the Elders

- Higher Beings (Song 4)

- Histories (Personal Histories, Song 5)

I

- Ikwiwghachi (Elder of Sound, Appendix A)

- Interdimensional Travel (Appendix B)

- Intergalactic Investigative Unit (Appendix C)

- Interactions (Higher Beings, Song 4)

J

- Justice (see Great Hall of Justice, Song 3)

K

- Knowledge (Realm of Knowledge, Appendix A)

- Korr (Agent, Character)

L

- Lila (Chosen Woman, Character)

- Linen (Healing Properties, Appendix B)

M

- Mmata (Elder of Dreams, Appendix A)

- Mmatachi (Elder of Emotions, Appendix A)

- Mmgbagwiw (Realm of Light, Appendix A)

- Mmgbar (Elder of Time, Appendix A)

- Mind (Realm of Mind, Appendix A)

- Multiverse (Appendix B)

N

- Nnaichi (Elder of Art, Appendix A)

- Nnaga (Elder of Space, Appendix A)

- Nnaka (Eldwer of Transformation, Appendix A)

- Nsa *also see Akwansa* (Elder of Darkness, Appendix A)

O

- Order (Cosmic Balance, Song 1)

P

- Personal Bonds (Song 5)

- Priestess Amina (Character)

- Prophecy (Chamber of Prophecy, Song 7)

- Purity (Linen, Appendix B)

Q

- Quantum Mechanics (Korr, Character)

- Quantum Entanglement (Appendix B)

R

- Realms (24 Realms, Appendix A)

- Remembrance (Hall of Remembrance, Song 10)

- Reporter (Character, Appendix A)

24: Universal Economics and the Song of the Elders

- Responsibilities (Elders, Chapter 2)

S

- Saraphina (Elder of Life, Appendix A)

- Shalara (Elder of Light, Appendix A)

- Space (Realm of Space, Appendix A)

- Spirits (Realm of Spirits, Appendix A)

- Superposition (Appendix B)

- Strategies (Council, Song 6)

- Succession (Legacy, Song 10)

T

- Taknnalanaza (Elder of Technology, Appendix A)

- Tazabah (Elder of Balance, Appendix A)

- Tazadaaka (Elder of Law, Appendix A)

- Transformation (Realm of Transformation, Appendix A)

24: Universal Economics and the Song of the Elders

U

- **Ulrich Von Sturm** (CERN Culprit, Character)

V

- Victim (Character,)

W

- Wadana (Elder of Flora, Appendix A)

- Wisdom (Song 7)

Z

- Zamarachi (Elder of Love, Appendix A)

- Zaphyr (Elder of Elements, Appendix A)

- Zara (Agent, Character)

Acknowledgements

First and foremost, I extend my deepest gratitude to Chi Akwa Aka Abiyah Mmaw Shi Ala and all my ancestors whose resilience and wisdom course through my veins, guiding me on this literary journey.

To my beloved sons, Abiyah Yasharahyalah, Tai-Zamarai Yasharahyalah (Junior), and Baraq (Chazariyah), your unwavering support and inspiration fuel my creativity and drive. You are my greatest blessings.

To my cherished wife and eternal companion, Naiyahmi Yasharahyalah, your love, encouragement, and unwavering belief in me have been the foundation upon which I've built my dreams. Daaliw for being my rock. This book is as much yours as it is mine.

About the Author

Tai-Zamarai Yasharahyalah is a multifaceted scholar and visionary, whose diverse expertise spans across genetics, ancient languages, nutrition, and life coaching. His unique background and interdisciplinary knowledge make him an authoritative voice in exploring the deep connections between science, spirituality, and the cosmic order.

Academic and Professional Background:

- *Medical Geneticist:* Tai-Zamarai is a distinguished medical geneticist, having graduated from Queen Mary University of London (QMUL). His research and insights into genetics have provided him with a profound understanding of the biological underpinnings of life, health, and human potential.

- *Certified Life Coach:* With certification from the International Coaching Federation (ICF), Tai-Zamarai is a seasoned life coach. He is dedicated to empowering individuals to achieve their highest potential through transformative guidance and personal development.

- *Ancient Languages Scholar:* As a universal student of ancient languages, Tai-Zamarai has a particular focus on Phoenician scripts and Ancient Hebrew. His in-depth knowledge of these languages allows him to uncover and interpret timeless wisdom from ancient texts, enriching his work with historical and spiritual insights.

- *Certified Plant-Based Nutritionist:* Tai-Zamarai's expertise in plant-based nutrition underscores his commitment to holistic health. He advocates for nutrition that aligns with both individual well-being and ecological sustainability.

Literary Contributions:

In his groundbreaking book, *24: Universal Economics and the Song of the Elders*, Tai-Zamarai weaves together his vast knowledge to explore the intricate dynamics that govern the multiverse. Through the lens of the Council of 24 Elders, he offers readers a profound journey into the universal principles that underpin existence, blending scientific rigor with spiritual depth.

Tai-Zamarai's work is characterized by its ability to challenge conventional thinking and inspire readers to explore new dimensions of knowledge and understanding. His interdisciplinary approach and holistic perspective make his contributions invaluable to those seeking to expand their consciousness and deepen their connection with the cosmos.

24: Universal Economics and the Song of the Elders

Vision and Mission:

Tai-Zamarai is committed to contributing to the collective evolution of consciousness. Through his writing, coaching, and educational efforts, he aims to foster a deeper understanding of the interconnectedness of all things and promote a more harmonious existence within the universal fabric of reality.

Embark on an extraordinary journey with *24: Universal Economics and the Song of the Elders* and uncover the timeless wisdom that shapes the fabric of reality, guided by the insightful and transformative vision of Tai-Zamarai Yasharahyalah.

Thanks for reading! Please add a short review on Amazon and let me know what you thought!

©B3 MAGNAT3

Printed in Great Britain
by Amazon

b963d60f-3d42-49ae-bb52-433997764b02R01